THE GUNSMITH

478

The Red Lady of San Francisco

THE GUNSMITH

478

The Red Lady of San Francisco

J. R. Roberts

SPEAKING VOLUMES, LLC
NAPLES, FLORIDA
2022

The Red Lady of San Francisco

ISBN 978-1-64540-768-3

Chapter One

Whenever the Gunsmith needed a dose of big city, it was usually Denver or San Francisco, as New York was too far to just drop in on.

This time it was San Francisco, where he could gamble and go to the theater. He spent almost as much time on the Barbary Coast as he did in Portsmouth Square at his friend Duke Farrell's casino and hotel: Duke's.

Clint had met Farrell through their mutual friend, Abel Tracker, and Tracker's recent death seemed to have brought them closer. Tracker had been killed while helping Clint with a job, causing Clint much guilt. But it was Duke who assured him that Tracker never did anything he didn't want to do. There was no need for him to feel guilty.

When Clint came to San Francisco, there was always a room waiting for him at Duke's. But since they were friends, when he gambled, he did it elsewhere. He had no desire to take money from Duke's pocket.

When he arrived at Duke's he boarded his Tobiano, who he had ridden to town rather than taking the train. He checked in, left his belongings in his room, and went down to find his friend. Duke spent his time in one of three places—his office, his casino, or the hotel restaurant.

On this day, he found Duke at his table in the restaurant, which Duke had named Tracker's.

"Goddamn!" Duke said, as Clint crossed the room to him.

Duke stood to his full five-foot-six and put his hand out to shake enthusiastically.

"Why didn't you tell me you were comin'?" Duke demanded.

"Then it wouldn't have been a surprise."

"Siddown and I'll get you a steak."

Clint sat as Duke waved the waiter over.

"Walter, bring a steak dinner for Mr. Adams before you bring mine."

"Yes, Sir."

"From my private stock," Duke added, pointing at the man.

"As you say, Sir."

"Private stock, huh?" Clint asked.

"Best beef in the state," Duke said.

"Good," Clint said. "I deserve it."

The waiter brought Clint a frothy mug of beer.

"What brings you here this time?" Duke asked, as Clint sipped.

"Just looking for some time to relax," Clint answered.

"You? Relax? That'll be the day."

"I mean it."

"You always mean it, but somethin' will come along—a friend in need, a damsel in distress. You can't keep your nose clean, Clint, and you know it."

"Not this time," Clint said. "I'm here to gamble, and maybe go to the theater."

"The theater," Duke said. "I've got just the place for you. It's called The Red Lady. It has several stages, and they put on various kinds of acts."

"Like what?"

"Everything from musicals to Shakespeare."

"Shakespeare is not on my list," Clint said, "but a musical would be very nice."

Walter came with both their meals and set the plates on the table.

"Tell me more about The Red Lady," Clint said, as they cut into their meat. Just the right amount of blood ran onto the plate.

"It opened only a month ago," Duke said. "I haven't been there myself yet, but I've heard only good things about it."

"I assume you can get me a ticket?"

"Of course," Duke said. "Tomorrow night?"

"Why not?"

"I'll see what shows they have. I'm sure there's a musical."

"That's fine."

"How's the steak?" Duke asked.

"Like you said," Clint answered. "Fine private stock."

"And for your gambling," Duke said, "elsewhere, as usual?"

"Definitely," Clint said. "The last thing I want to do is break your bank."

"It could still be half your bank, Clint," Duke said. "Partners?"

"I don't think so, Duke," Clint said. "I really don't want to have that kind of responsibility."

"You could be a wealthy man."

"All I need is enough money to keep moving," Clint said.

"And in the event one day you decide to settle down?" Duke asked.

"If that day ever comes," Clint said, "you'll be the first I tell."

Chapter Two

Clint decided not to gamble that night. He was tired from riding for days and thought he would get a good night's sleep. So after dinner with Duke, he went to his room, stripped down to his skivvies and took out the book he was currently reading: WAVERLY, by Sir Walter Scott. Because Scott did not take credit for those books until 1827, they were published as a series of "Waverly" novels. This was the first in the series, published in 1814.

He sat on the bed with his gunbelt on the bedpost and read until his eyes started to droop. Then he closed the book, doused the light and went to sleep.

***

He woke the next morning at nine, which was later than usual. Maybe he was getting too old for late nights, even spent reading.

He had breakfast alone in the dining room, served by a different waiter who, nevertheless, knew who he was.

"Ham-and-eggs, coffee," Clint said.

"Yes, Mr. Adams."

The waiter left and returned with a pot of coffee. Soon Clint had his breakfast and was enjoying it. It was so much better than jerky and beans on the trail. He forgot how much he liked the food in San Francisco, in addition to the gambling and other diversions.

He ate his breakfast at a leisurely pace, going through, in his mind, his choices of casinos. There was The Parker House, Samuel Dennison's Exchange, The El Dorado, and many more, including some of his favorites, The St. Charles, The Alhambra and The Bella Union.

He tried to put them in the order he would visit them, an order he would pursue unless he found an interesting enough private poker game.

He had not played much serious poker in recent months, sticking to penny ante games just to pass the time, but he was in the heart of gambling, where many of the big names could be found. He thought he might even run into Bat Masterson or Luke Short. Poker with those two good friends was always challenging, but a pleasure at the same time.

He decided Duke would know if his friends were in town, so he would ask him before he left.

After breakfast he asked the desk clerk where he could find Duke.

"He's in his office, Sir. He said you should go right back, any time."

"Thanks," Clint said.

He knocked on the door, and when Duke shouted, "Come ahead!" he found the man seated behind his huge, cherry wood desk.

"My God, that looks even bigger than the last time I was here."

"It is," Duke said. "It's a new desk. Have a seat. I don't have your tickets yet, it's too early."

"That's okay," Clint said. "I was thinking about poker, and that made me wonder if Bat or Luke were in town."

"Not that I know of," Duke said. "I don't think there's a big enough game goin' on now to entice them."

"Well, I don't need a high roller game, just something more than penny ante. I'm a little out of practice, anyway."

"I can put together a game, if you like," Duke said. "Any stakes, you name it."

"Naw," Clint said, "I'll go casino to casino and see what I can find. I'm sure there'll be something interesting out there."

"There always is," Duke confirmed. "But you won't find much during the daylight hours."

Clint stood up.

"I'll while away the time with Blackjack and Roulette."

"No Faro?"

Clint made a face.

"Faro's not a favorite of mine."

"Still? You won't have Wyatt Earp to go up against, you know."

"I know that," Clint said. "I don't even know where Wyatt is now, but I'm sure I won't find him here."

"There are some big gamblers in town," Duke said. "Brady, Brett, Ben Silver—"

"I don't know him," Clint said.

"If you haven't been playin' lately, you wouldn't. He's come along just recently and made a name for himself against some of the best, like Luke, and Dandy Jim Buckley."

"Has he played against Bat?"

"I don't know, but I think he's sat across from Hawkes a time or two."

"Well, maybe I'll run into him," Clint said, standing. "I'm going to walk around the Square for a while."

"Come back for dinner and I'll have your ticket by then," Duke said.

"I'll see you this evening," Clint said, and went out to try his luck in Portsmouth Square.

Chapter Three

The casinos were open early, but games were not yet going hot and heavy. Clint saved the better casinos, and his favorites, for later in the day, when they would be busy. He went into several during the afternoon, played some Blackjack and Roulette, even tried his luck at the Wheel of Fortune. By the time late afternoon came along, he was hungry, and a couple of hundred dollars ahead, mostly due to the fact that he never lost more than two hands of Blackjack in a row and was dealt Blackjack several times.

He decided to have a late lunch outside of Duke's hotel and picked a small café that he had been to before. He did not recognize any of the waiters, but the food was just as good as it ever was.

When he returned to the hotel, Duke was on the casino floor, according to the desk clerk.

"He walks it every afternoon, and then spends each evening there."

"I don't want to bother him while he's working," Clint said.

"That's all right, Sir," the clerk said. "He left this for you." The young man handed him an envelope. Inside were two tickets to shows at the Red Lady Theater.

"Thank you," Clint said.

"He also wanted me to tell you that the Red Lady has a variety of entertainment available: gambling, a restaurant and a saloon."

"Everything a man could want," Clint said.

"And more."

"Have you ever been there?"

"Me? No, Sir. I stay away from places like that."

"Okay," Clint said, holding up the envelope, "thanks for these."

He went to his room to dress for an evening of gambling, dining and entertainment.

***

He decided to save his visits to places like the Alhambra and the Exchange for the next night, and caught a horse drawn cab in front of the hotel.

"Do you know where the Red Lady is?" he asked the driver.

"Everybody does, Sir," the man said.

"Take me there."

"Yes, Sir."

The ride from Portsmouth Square to the Barbary Coast was not a long one. It took Clint right through the center of Chinatown. The restaurants, laundries and odors were all familiar. Chinese men and women were scurrying about, in the midst of their daily chores.

When the driver pulled up in front of The Red Lady Clint was impressed. It was the largest theater he had ever seen, taking up the better part of two blocks. There were several entrances, but the one the cab dropped him in front of was framed in ornate gold, with large blazing red letters above it that said THE RED LADY.

He paid the driver and thanked him, then approached the door. There was a large black man, clad in black, blocking the way.

"Good evening, Sir," he said. "Do you have a ticket? You need a ticket to enter through this door."

"I have two tickets," Clint said, "for two different shows, I think."

The man looked at Clint's tickets. "Oh, no, Sir. One ticket gets you into the building. The other ticket gets you into the show."

"I see."

"I'll take this one," the man said, "and you can go in."

"Thank you."

"And Sir?"

"Yes?"

"Are you carrying a weapon?"

Clint was not wearing his Peacemaker in a holster, but he did have his Colt New Line tucked into his belt.

"I am," he said, and lifted his jacket tails to show it.

"I'll have to ask for that, Sir."

"You can ask," Clint said, "but you can't have it."

"Sir?"

"I said no."

The man stretched himself to his full six-foot-six, probably thinking it would intimidate Clint.

"May I ask why, Sir?"

"Because I never go anywhere unarmed."

"Sir, I can't let you in here with a gun."

"Is there someone I can talk to?"

The man frowned at Clint for a moment. "Can I ask who you are?"

"Yes," Clint said, "my name's Clint Adams."

It was obvious that struck a chord with the man.

"If you'll give me a minute, Mr. Adams?" he asked.

"Sure," Clint said, "take your time, as long as I don't miss the show."

The man nodded, went inside, and returned a few minutes later. He held the door open.

"Go right in, Sir," he said. "Have a pleasant night."

"Thank you," Clint said, and entered.

Chapter Four

He found himself in a large lobby, floor and walls covered in red. Crystal chandeliers hung from a high ceiling. A young lady in a purple dress approached him.

"Welcome, Sir," she said. "Are you here to eat, drink, gamble, or attend the theater?"

"Well," Clint said, "why don't I just try all four?"

"May I see your ticket?"

He showed it to her.

"This show doesn't start for two hours," she said. "I can seat you in our restaurant immediately."

"That sounds good," he said. "I'm hungry."

"This way, please."

She walked ahead of him, hips swaying, and he followed. All the hallways were red.

"What's your name?" he asked.

"Delilah."

"Why aren't you dressed in red, Delilah?"

She looked at him over her shoulder and said, "Because I'm not the Red Lady."

"You mean there really is a red lady?" Clint asked.

"Oh, yes," Delilah said, "and she's the only one who wears red. The rest of us can wear any other color we want."

She stopped in front of a wide door.

"Here we are. What kind of table would you prefer?"

"Something in the back," he said.

She turned and looked at him, smiled her lovely smile.

"How far back?"

"Way back," he said, "preferably with my back to the wall."

"My, my," she said. "Follow me."

She waved a man in a tuxedo away as they crossed the room to the furthest table from the door.

"Will this do?"

"Perfectly."

"Are you an adventurous eater?" she asked. "Or do you want a steak, like every other man?"

"I like steak," he said, "but I also like adventure."

"Good," she said. "I'll order for you. Please, enjoy your meal."

"Can't you join me?"

"I'm afraid not," she said, "but I'll be back to take you to the saloon for a drink, after, before the show."

"I'll look forward to it."

She smiled and walked across the room. When she went through another door, he assumed it led to the kitchen. He settled back to wait and watch the other diners.

***

Delilah went into the kitchen, placed Clint's order, then continued on through another door. She took a hallway to a closed door, knocked and entered.

"Delilah," the lady behind the desk said, "did you make Mr. Adams comfortable?"

"Yes, I did," Delilah said. "He's in the dining room waiting for his dinner."

"Good, very good," the lady in the red dress said. "I want him to enjoy himself."

"I'm wondering," Delilah said, "if he's the Gunsmith, is he here to shoot somebody?"

"Oh, I doubt it," the woman said. "He can find a lot of other places to do something like that."

"I guess you're right."

"So, what's he like, this Gunsmith?"

"He's a gentleman," Delilah said. "He's wearing a suit, not a gun. He doesn't look like a gunfighter."

"And?"

"And he's very good looking."

"Well, that's his reputation," the red lady said. "Which show does he have a ticket for?"

"Miss Daisy's."

"Change it."

"To what?"

"Sit him in the audience for my show."

"Your show is full, Ma'am."

"I don't care," she said. "Give him a front row seat. I want to get a good look at him."

"Yes, Ma'am."

As Delilah started for the door, the red lady said, "Delilah?"

"Yes, Ma'am?"

"Did he ask you to dine with him?"

"Yes, Ma'am."

"What did you tell him?"

"I said I couldn't, but I'd be back to take him to the saloon."

"That's good," she said. "If he asks you to have a drink with him, say yes. And answer all his questions."

"Yes, Ma'am."

"And make sure he gets a good meal," the red lady added. "I want him to be a happy man."

"He will be, Ma'am," Delilah said.

"And if wants to fuck you—"

Delilah's eyes flashed.

"Don't be impudent!"

"I'm sorry," the red lady said. "I got carried away."

Delilah turned and left.

Chapter Five

When the waiter brought his dinner Clint asked, "What have we here?"

"Duck breast, Sir," the waiter said. "It's our chef's specialty, cooked in a plum sauce."

"It looks interesting," Clint admitted, eyeing the large breast surrounded by various vegetables.

"Anything else, Sir?"

"I'd like a beer to wash this down," Clint said.

"Right away, Sir."

The waiter went off and, as promised, came back right away with a beer.

"Thanks," Clint said. "That's all."

The man walked away, and Clint cut into the succulent breast and tasted it. The plum sauce was sweet, but not too much so. After the first bite, Clint consumed the rest of the meal with relish.

He had just finished when Delilah put in another appearance.

"How was it?" she asked.

"Delicious."

"Are you ready for a visit to our saloon?"

"Lead the way."

Once again, he followed her swinging hips down red-lined hallways until they reached a large saloon. At that point, the predominance of red was no surprise.

For a saloon with no girls, no music and no gambling, it was doing a brisk business.

She led him to the bar and asked, "Whiskey?"

"Beer," he said.

She called the bartender over. "A beer for Mister Adams, Bennett. And the regular for me."

"Yes, Ma'am."

When he had a mug of beer in his hand, and she a glass of champagne, she asked, "Would you like to do some gambling after this?"

"You have a casino here, too?"

"We have a little bit of everything," she told him.

"I think gambling will have to wait until after the show, don't you?"

"Yes, of course," she said. "I almost forgot. It should be starting in about twenty minutes. Time enough to finish our drinks."

"Tell me something, Delilah."

"Anything."

"How do I rate all this attention from someone as beautiful as you?"

"You presented yourself at our front door," she said. "A famous man, a legend of the West. We only want to show you a good time."

"And who made that decision?"

"Why, the Red Lady herself."

"And will I get to meet the Red Lady, herself?"

"Who knows?" Delilah said. "Maybe we'll see, after the show. Follow me, and I'll take you to your seat."

They finished their drinks and Delilah once again led him down a labyrinth of red hallways until they passed through a curtained doorway into a crowded theater. There were many seats, and they all seemed to be filled. At the front of the large room was a wide, raised stage.

Delilah led him down an aisle to a seat in the first row.

"A front row seat," he said. "I don't think I rate this."

"Sit and enjoy," Delilah said. "I'll see you after the show."

"I thought this was supposed to be some kind of play," he said, looking at the empty stage.

"We changed your ticket," she said, "I think you'll enjoy this."

She withdrew and, as if on cue, music began to play and out onto the stage came a lady dressed in red.

Chapter Six

She had long, flowing red hair that came down over her bare shoulders. The red gown she wore extended down to the floor and, from where he sat, with her up on the stage, she looked to be six feet tall.

So this was the Red Lady.

When she opened her mouth and began to sing, he forgot everything else and was carried away with the rest of the audience. But before he knew it, she was finished and vanished amidst clamorous applause.

"How was it?"

He looked up and saw Delilah standing there, as the audience filed out around her.

"She was amazing," he admitted. "That *was* her, wasn't it? The Red Lady, herself?"

"That was her."

"She came out with no introduction," Clint said. "How do people know who she is?"

"Everyone knows the Red Lady," Delilah said. "Would you like to meet her?"

"I would, very much," he said.

"Come with me, then."

They followed the crowd from the theater. As the people made their way to the dining room, or saloon, or casino, or even to the front door to go home, Delilah took him down the longest corridor yet, to a closed door, upon which she knocked.

"Come in," a voice called.

Delilah opened the door and said, "Mr. Adams, Ma'am."

"Oh, please, send him in," the voice said.

Delilah stepped aside and said, "Please, go in."

"Thank you."

He went through the door, which Delilah closed behind him. A woman was seated in front of a mirrored dressing table. She stood and turned to face him, holding a red robe closed with one hand. The other hand she extended to him. Standing this close, as opposed to looking up at her on stage, she was still a tall woman, probably five ten, or so.

"It's a pleasure to meet you, Mr. Adams."

He stepped forward and shook the proffered hand.

"You have me at a disadvantage," he said. "Do I simply refer to you as Red Lady?"

She laughed, and it was as melodious as her singing had been.

"My name is Genevieve," she said. "My last name doesn't really matter."

"If you say so."

"Please, have a seat," she said.

There were two comfortable looking easy chairs in the room. He sat in one, and she in the other.

"Do you treat all your new customers this way?" he asked.

"Heavens, no," she said, "only the infamous ones."

"So, Bat Masterson would get the same treatment?"

"Of course. Although I probably would have had Delilah take him to the casino and not to my show."

"Believe me," Clint said, "Bat would have enjoyed your performance as much as I did."

"You know him?"

"We're good friends."

"Are all legends also friends?" she asked, looking amused.

"Just some," he said.

She sat back in her chair and crossed her legs.

"So, what do you think of the place?"

"It's amazing," he said, "what I've seen of it."

"Oh yes, you've yet to see the casino," she said. "I'll have Delilah take you there next."

"How long have you been open?" he asked. "I heard it hasn't been long."

"Two months, I think."

"And you seem to have built up quite a clientele in that short time."

"People are curious," she said. "And once they've been here, they come back."

"I can see why," he said. "And then there's your, well, imposing figure. I mean, calling yourself the Red Lady. I assume you don't introduce yourself to many people by name."

"That's quite right," she said. "I like being the mysterious Red Lady."

"Why did you choose the Barbary Coast for your location, and not Portsmouth Square?"

"Oh," she said, rolling her eyes, "the competition in Portsmouth Square . . . well, I'm sure you've been to many of those places."

"I have," he said, "but this place would stand up to any of them."

"Well," she said, "believe it or not, this property was not very expensive. You should have seen it when I bought it. Most of the money I spent was in renovations."

"Well, it all seems to have been worth it," he said.

"Wait til you see the casino," she said, standing. "I'll have Delilah take you there. Will you join me for a drink later?"

"I'd be happy to," he said.

She went to the door to get Delilah.

Chapter Seven

The casino was as impressive, if not more so, then the rest of the place. It would take time to decide if the dealers and equipment were the equal of some Portsmouth Square operations, but at first sight it seemed likely.

"We have every game possible," Delilah told him. "And a bar in the corner, if you get thirsty while playing."

"I don't drink while gambling, but thanks," Clint said.

"Would you like me to take you around?"

"I think I can manage that myself," Clint said.

"If you need me, just ask anyone to send for me, and I'll be here."

"Thank you, Delilah," Clint said.

She smiled and backed away. In seconds she had disappeared into the crowd.

Clint decided to take a stroll around the entire operation before doing any gambling. He wanted to observe some of the dealers to make sure everything was on the up-and-up. After a good hour spent watching, he decided to play some Blackjack.

While playing, he heard some conversations about the actual "Red Lady." Several then seemed to believe she was a high-priced whore. Others thought the whole operation was a front for a high-priced bordello. Clint's one meeting with the woman gave him no standing to argue the point, but he was forced to wonder. So far, Delilah had made no mention of supplying him with a woman for the night, or even offering herself.

After an hour or so of playing even, Clint decided to move on. He gave the roulette wheel a try, while listening to more conversations. The general opinion of both men and women was that the Red Lady was a whore. Clint wondered what Genevieve had done to foster such opinions? He might have to ask Delilah for some information.

He left the table after half-an-hour, still having played even. Making his way to the corner bar, he ordered a beer, turned his back, leaned against the bar, and watched the activities. There were no women there without escorts. He wondered if that was a rule? Something else he would ask Delilah.

He turned and waved to the bartender.

"Another, Sir?"

"No, thanks," he said. "Could you fetch Delilah for me?"

"Of course, Sir," the bartender said. "She'll be right along."

He finished his beer while he waited. Before long she appeared, still in her purple dress, and stood next to him.

"Finished already?" she asked. "Did you take us for that much?"

"Actually," he said, "I played even."

"So you're calling it a night?"

"As far as gambling is concerned."

"What else is there?" she asked. "I think you've seen everything we have to offer."

"Have I?"

"What do you think you haven't seen?"

"I've heard a lot of talk in this room," he told her.

"There's always talk," she said. "What have you heard?"

"A lot of unpleasant comments about the Red Lady."

"Our operation?" she asked. "Or the Red Lady, herself?"

"Both, actually."

"Ah," Delilah said. "I think I know what you mean. Why don't we go someplace more quiet to talk?"

He put his empty mug down on the bar and said, "Lead the way."

***

She took him to a table in a quiet corner of the saloon. With no gambling, no music and no girls working the floor, it was a perfect location for a quiet discussion.

"So you've heard the talk about a high-priced bordello," she said.

"Yes."

"And you believed it?"

"I don't have enough information to believe or disbelieve it," Clint said. "That's why I wanted to talk to you."

"So ask your questions."

"Is a bordello part of your operation?"

"No."

"So there's no sex for sale."

"We have girls who work for us," she said. "It's up to them if they want to entertain or not. We don't employ them to do so."

"I see."

"So if you were expecting to have sex with me—"

"That thought never crossed my mind," he said, interrupting her."

"Really?"

"First of all," he said, "I never pay for sex."

"Never?"

"I never have, and never will," he told her.

"And what's second?"

"Second?"

"You said 'first of all,'" she reminded him. "What's second?"

"Well," he said, "I heard talk that Genevieve herself might be a prostitute, a very high-priced prostitute."

"Are you asking me if the Red Lady is a whore?"

"No, I'm not," he said. "I'm saying I don't believe she is."

"That's good, because she isn't." She paused, then added, "And neither am I."

Chapter Eight

When Delilah's purple dress hit the floor, she stood before him in her frilly underwear, which was also purple.

She told him she had a room on the top floor, above the theater and casino.

"Several of us do," she said. "It's up to us if we want to take anyone up there."

"And?" he asked.

"I'd like to take you up there," she said.

He smiled, and they left the saloon together.

Now he watched her divest herself of her frilly underthings, until she stood naked before him. She was medium height, full breasts and hips, which her clothing had hidden fairly well. Fully dressed, she was a lovely woman. Naked, with her auburn hair down around her shoulders, and long enough to hide her nipples, she appeared bawdy. Especially her smile . . .

He approached her, brushed her long hair aside so he could touch her nipples, which made her close her eyes and bite her lower lip.

Then he kissed her, and her tongue darted avidly into his mouth. During the kiss she peeled his jacket off and tossed it aside, then unbuttoned his shirt and slid her hands inside. As the kiss continued, she slid one hand down over the bulge in his trousers, and when she tried to undo his trousers, encountered his gun.

"Oh," she said. "I don't think that will be necessary."

"I'll set it over here," he said, and placed it on the night table next to the bed, where he could reach it if the need arose.

From there she found it very easy to undress him and toss his boots aside. When he was fully nude, she gave all her attention to his hardening cock. She fell to her knees, took him into her mouth and suckled him until he was fully rigid. Then she stood, took his hand and led him to her bed.

When they were on her bed together, he pushed her down onto her back and began to explore her flesh with his mouth and tongue. He worked his way down until his face was nestled between her thighs, and then went to work on her until she was writhing on the bed as waves of pleasure flowed over her and through her . . .

***

"I hope you don't think I was instructed to do this," she said. "I was told to show you all the entertainments we have, but this wasn't included."

"I accept that," he said.

"I wondered about this from the moment we met," she said. "And, of course, I admit who you are had something to do with it. I hope you won't think badly of me because of that."

"Not at all," he said.

She was stroking his cock gently, but as it swelled again, she stopped and said, "I'm sorry, but we have to go."

"Go?"

"I'm still working," she said. She stood and began dressing. "I can take you back to the casino, or the saloon—"

"No," he said, swinging his feet to the floor, "that's okay. I'm ready to go back to my hotel."

They both got dressed, and he gave her time to pin her hair back in place. Then she led him to the front door.

"I hope I'll see you again," she said.

"I think you can count on that," he said. "I was very entertained tonight."

She actually blushed and smiled, the large doorman closing the door behind him.

"I hope you had a good time, Sir," the man said.

"I had a very good time, thanks."

"Can I get you a cab?"

"Please."

***

Three men stood across the street, waiting for the doorman to be occupied. When he was calling for a cab for a customer who was leaving, they hurried across the street. The Red Lady was made up of two buildings, which had a very narrow alleyway between them. The three men took the alley to the rear of the building, carrying torches with them.

When they reached the back, they searched for a likely location to do what they had been hired to do.

"I hate this job," one of them said. "I was here, once. It's real nice."

"Yeah, well," another man said, "looks like somebody thinks it's too nice."

"Let's stop talkin' about it and just get it done," the third man said. "You two keep goin' and find two more places. When you're ready, light your torches and signal me. We've gotta do this at the same time, and then get away from here."

"Right," the other two said.

They moved on, while the third man lit his torch and waited for the signal.

Chapter Nine

Clint woke the next morning and went down to the dining room for breakfast. Duke was already at his table, so he joined him.

"I'll have whatever he's having," he told the waiter.

"Very good, Sir."

Clint was pleasantly surprised to find that it was steak-and-eggs.

"Every so often I treat myself," Duke said. "Did you go to the Red Lady last night?"

"I did."

"And the show?"

"It was very good," Clint said. "They gave me a front row seat to hear the Red Lady perform."

"Really!" Duke said. "That's not the ticket I bought you."

"I know, but in order to keep my gun I had to tell the doorman who I was."

"Ah," Duke said, "so once they heard that, they treated you like royalty."

"Exactly."

"Letting the public know the Gunsmith was there and enjoyed himself would be very helpful to them, bringing a new clientele."

"It seemed to me they had plenty," Clint said. "For a place that's been open only two months, they seem to be doing quite well."

"They were until last night," Duke said.

"What happened last night?"

"It must have been after you left," Duke said. "They had a fire."

"What? How bad?"

"It could've been worse," Duke said. "They managed to put it out quickly, but somebody set it."

"What?" Clint said. "Why would they do that?"

"That place is stiff competition, Clint," Duke said. "Not everyone is happy about it being there."

"Did they catch the firebugs?"

"No, they have no idea who set the fire."

"Was anyone hurt?"

"Don't think so."

"You know, I met her last night."

"Who? The Red Lady?"

Clint nodded.

"She's very impressive," Clint said. "And from what I heard and saw, she's imposing."

"What were people saying?"

"Mostly, that she's a whore," Clint said. "Talking that way about her, you can tell she intimidates people."

"That's what I heard," Duke said. "So now that you met her, you want to help her, right?"

"She didn't ask for any help," Clint said.

"That's never stopped you from helping a beautiful woman."

"Have you ever seen her?"

"No."

"Then how do you know she's beautiful?"

"First, that's what I've heard," Duke said, "and second, I see the look on your face."

"Well," Clint said, "I'm sorry someone set her place on fire, but she hasn't asked me my help, so I'm going to mind my own business."

"What was your favorite part of last night?" Duke asked.

Clint didn't mention the time he spent with Delilah in her room.

"The show was very good, and so was the casino. Also, I had a very interesting meal."

"Oh? What was it?"

"Duck breast in plum sauce," Clint said. "Very good."

"It sounds good," Duke said. "I'll have to ask our chef to try it."

"That's a good idea."

"Did they give you anything else you think we could use?" Duke asked.

"No," Clint said, "nothing at all."

He turned his attention to his breakfast.

***

The three men who had set the fire at the Red Lady stood in front of the man who had hired them.

You obviously did a half-assed job," the man said.

"We thought we did a good enough job to get the deed done," one of the men said. "We didn't know that a waiter would spot the flames and raise the alarm."

"We can try again," one of the other men said.

"You won't," their boss said. "I paid you all for a job and you didn't do it. I want you to use that money to leave town."

"Leave San Francisco?" the third man asked. "And go where?"

"Anywhere," their boss said. "Just go."

"And when do we come back?" the first man asked. "This is our home."

"I'll contact you when you can return," the boss said. "Just let me know where you are."

"Sir—"

"Just go!" the boss snapped. "I'll find somebody else who can do the job properly."

Chapter Ten

After breakfast Duke said he had some business to attend to. Clint told him to go ahead, he would be able to entertain himself. But when they came out of the dining room, Clint realized he wouldn't have to. Delilah was waiting in the lobby for him. Duke had never met Delilah, so didn't know she was representing the Red Lady.

"I'll leave you to your guest," Duke said, and headed for his office.

Clint walked over to where Delilah stood.

"Good morning," he greeted. "I hope everyone is okay after last night's scare."

"That's what I'm here to talk to you about," Delilah admitted. "Is there somewhere quiet we can talk?"

"We could go to my room," he said.

"I'm afraid we might not get much talking done if we did that," she suggested.

"Then let's try the bar," Clint said. "It shouldn't be busy at this hour."

"That suits me," she said.

They sat at a back table in the empty saloon, with cups of coffee in front of them.

"Obviously, you've heard about the fires."

"Fires?" Clint asked. "There were more than one?"

"Three," she said, "in three different parts of the building. Luckily, one of our waiters stepped out back for some air and saw the flames. He raised the alarm and the fire brigade was there in minutes."

"How did Genevieve take it?"

"Not too well," Delilah said. "That's why I'm here. I told her she needs help and suggested you. She said no."

"So you're here on your own?"

"Clint," Delilah said, "this isn't the first time somebody's tried something. In fact, it was just a few weeks ago somebody tried to kill her."

"Oh? How?"

"They tried to make it look like an accident, like she had been run down in the street by an out-of-control horse and carriage."

"Has she talked to the law?"

"Genevieve doesn't want to get involved with the law," Delilah said.

"Why not?"

"Let's just say that everything at the Red Lady is not exactly on the up-and-up."

"But if someone tried to kill her and burn her out—"

"She says she can handle everything herself."

"Does she say how?"

"No," Delilah said, "she just tells me not to worry."

"What's your position in the Red Lady, Delilah?"

"I suppose you'd say I'm her right hand lady."

"Does she ask for your advice?" Clint asked.

"No," Delilah said, "she doesn't ask anyone for advice."

"So what's she going to think of you coming to see me?" Clint asked.

"She's not gonna like it." Delilah admitted, "but we need help, and we need it from someone like you."

Clint stared across the table at her. He had been determined to come to San Francisco, mind his own business, and enjoy himself. Now he was being asked to jump right into someone else's problem.

"Will you do it?" Delilah asked.

"I'll tell you what I'll do," he said. "I'll talk with Genevieve and see how she feels about it. Then I'll make up my mind, if she asks for help."

"I'm so afraid she won't," Delilah said, "but okay, if that's the way you want to do it."

Clint walked Delilah to the front door.

"I'll come by tonight and present myself to the doorman."

"I'll see to it that he lets you in."

"Wait," Clint said. "Tell me about the doorman."

"His name is Honey Roy DuPre," she said. "He's from New Orleans."

"How did he get the job?"

"Genevieve felt she needed a big man on the door," Delilah said. "She knew Honey from when he was a fighter."

"He doesn't seem like a punch-drunk fighter to me."

"He's not," she said. "He's got a brain."

"Then maybe she should be getting better use out of him," Clint said.

"I agree."

"All right," he said. "Go back to the Red Lady and don't tell Genevieve I'm coming."

"I won't."

"And Delilah, I don't want you to come outside by yourself anymore."

"You think someone might try to hurt me?" she asked.

"What better way to get to the head lady than by taking out her number one?" Clint asked. "Apparently, nobody's thought of that, yet."

"Including me," Delilah said, "but now I have, and it scares me."

"Good," Clint said. "The best way to stay alive is to stay scared."

Chapter Eleven

Clint found Duke in his office.

"Something up?" Duke asked.

"Maybe," Clint said. "How much do you know about somebody trying to kill the Red Lady? The place and the woman?"

"I heard there was a close call where she could have gotten hurt. Something about a runaway carriage."

"So you haven't heard anything about somebody wanting her dead?"

"No, why," Duke asked, "have you?"

"Apparently," Clint said, "last night's fires were just the next in a long line of attempts."

"Fires? More than one."

"Yes, three of them."

"Jesus!"

"The lady I just spoke to in the lobby works at the Red Lady, and says they need help."

"And they're asking you."

"Yes," Clint said, and then "don't say it!"

"I'm not saying a word."

"I'm going to go by there tonight and talk to the Red Lady," Clint said. "Apparently, she's determined to handle everything herself."

"But this other lady doesn't think she can?"

"Doesn't think she should," Clint said. "I guess I'll find out."

"I guess you will."

Clint started to leave, then turned back.

"You remember a man named Honey Roy DuPre?"

"A fighter, wasn't he? And a good one, if I remember correctly."

"That's what I heard."

"I also seem to remember that Bat Masterson once refereed one of his fights."

"That's right," Clint said. "Now I remember."

"Why'd you ask about him?"

"He's working at the Red Lady."

"As what?"

"A doorman."

"Seems his talents could be put to better use."

"Probably."

"Let me know how it goes tonight," Duke said.

"I'll do that," Clint said, "but I'm going to do some gambling in the better houses between now and then."

"Good," Duke said, "take them for all they're worth."

***

As it turned out, Clint took them for a bit more, but he ran into poker player Ben Silver in Sam Dennison's Exchange.

"Let me buy you a drink at the bar," Silver said.

"That suits me."

When they were standing at the bar with a beer each Silver asked, "Are you in town for some poker?"

"I was," Clint said, "but things may be changing."

"Oh? How so?"

Silver was in his late forties and had been making a living with the pasteboards long enough to have played with the likes of Hickok, Doc Holliday and Poker Alice. He was tall, broad shouldered, and just happened to have a streak of silver in his black hair.

"What do you know about the Red Lady?" Clint asked.

"New place in town, making a name for itself. The Red Lady also owns and operates it."

"Seems like there are those in town who don't like the competition."

"I can see why," Silver said. "It offers pretty much everything. Some folks even think there's a high-priced bordello on the top floor. What's your interest in the workers?"

"I was there last night and met some of the people who work there."

"Including the Red Lady, herself?"

"I did meet her, as a matter of fact, after I saw her show."

"She's quite a beauty."

"Yes, she is."

"Are you and she an item?"

"No, nothing like that," Clint said. "You heard about the fires last night?"

"I know," Silver said. "Sounds like she was pretty lucky."

"How long have you been in town?" Clint asked.

"A few weeks."

"So you probably heard about some of the other things that happened."

"I heard she almost got run down in the street," Silver said. "Is she thinking that was deliberate?"

"Well, the fires certainly were," Clint said.

"Wait," Silver said, "is she trying to bring you in on this?"

"As a matter of fact, she isn't," Clint said. "She seems to feel she can handle it, herself."

"But you don't?"

"Someone who works for her has asked me to get involved."

"I guess if anyone can get to the bottom of the problem, it's you," Silver said. He took out his watch and looked at it. "Hey, I'm late for a game." He finished his beer. "Clint, if you find you need any help, call on me. I'm staying at The Parker House."

"Thanks, Ben," Clint said. "I'll keep that in mind. And thanks for the drink."

Chapter Twelve

When Clint arrived at the Red Lady, Honey Roy DuPre was on the door.

"Good evenin', Mr. Adams."

" 'evening, Honey Roy."

"How'd you know my name?" the big man asked.

"I saw you fight once," Clint said. "I believe Bat Masterson was the referee."

"I remember that fight," Honey Roy said. "I knocked Moose Malone out in the eighth round."

"You should have gotten a shot at the title after that," Clint said. "What happened?"

"I was supposed to throw that fight," Honey Roy said. "I didn't."

"And they made you pay."

"Not only did I not get a shot at the title," Honey Roy said, "I never got another fight."

"You look like you could still take the title," Clint said.

"I'd have to get an early knockout," Honey Roy said. "I'm forty-eight, now."

"You look like you're in your prime," Clint said.

"Thanks for that," Honey Roy said. "Would you like to go in?"

"I would," Clint said. "I'd like to see Delilah."

"Step inside," Honey Roy said. "I'll find her."

"Thanks."

Clint went through the door into the red-lined lobby and waited. It was only minutes later that Delilah appeared in her purple gown.

"You came," she said.

"I told you I would."

"Good," she said, "we'll talk to Genevieve together."

"Have you told her I was coming?"

"No," she said.

"So it'll be a surprise."

"Don't worry," Delilah said, "I'll tell her it was my idea."

"Will she fire you?"

"I doubt it. Come, she's in her office."

He followed her down the winding halls to a solid door, upon which she knocked.

"Come!"

Delilah opened the door and said, "Clint Adams is here."

"Send him in," Clint heard the Red Lady say.

Delilah stepped aside to allow Clint to enter, then walked in behind him and closed the door."

Genevieve, in her red gown, was seated behind her desk.

"Mr. Adams," she asked, smiling, "what brings you here today?"

"Well—" Clint started, but Delilah interrupted him.

"I asked him to come," she said. "We need his help."

Genevieve looked at Delilah and asked, "With what?"

"You know what, Genevieve."

"I told you, Delilah; I'll handle the problem myself."

"You can fire me for saying this if you want," Delilah said, "but you're fooling yourself if you think that. These people want you dead."

"That was an accident!"

"It wasn't!"

"Suppose you tell me what's been going on," Clint suggested.

"You can go, Delilah," Genevieve said. "We'll talk about this later."

"Whatever you say," Delilah said, and left.

"You're not going to fire her, are you?" Clint asked.

"I'd never fire her," the Red Lady said, "but she shouldn't have brought you into this."

"Since I'm here," Clint said, "why not ask my advice."

"Very well," she said. "Sit, please."

Clint sat in front of her desk.

"Can I offer you a drink?"

"It's a little early for me."

"Coffee, then?"

"Thank you."

There was a pot on a sideboard. She walked to it and poured two cups, handed Clint one and then sat.

"What advice do you think I need?"

"Tell me what you're up against."

"I don't really know," she said.

"Then my advice is to find out," Clint said.

"There are those who begrudge me my success," she said. "They've tried several times to do me, or my business, harm."

"And they'll probably keep trying until you stop them," Clint said. "How do you propose to do that?"

She hesitated a moment, then said, "I don't know."

"Delilah said you told her you'd handle it."

"I've always handled my own business," she said.'

"This isn't the same thing?"

"I suppose Delilah told you I need help."

"Three fires last night," Clint said. "I'd say you need help."

"And you're offering?"

"No," Clint said. "I told Delilah I would come and talk to you. After that, you would have to ask for my help. And even then, there's no guarantee I'll say yes."

"All right," she relented. "It started even before we opened . . ."

Chapter Thirteen

Clint listened in silence while Genevieve laid out the odds she had been dealing with.

"So, for the most part, it's been someone trying to sabotage your business."

"Until they tried to kill me."

"The runaway wagon?"

"It was deliberate," she said. "I have no doubt."

"Then if you believe someone is trying to kill you," Clint said, "you have to *know* you can defend yourself. If not, then you need help."

"So you want me to ask for yours," she said.

"It doesn't matter who you ask," Clint said. "Staying alive when someone wants you dead is not a task to be taken lightly."

"You think I'm foolish to try and handle it myself?" she asked.

"Very."

"As you would—what? Become my bodyguard?"

"That depends."

"On what?"

"On what you want me to do," Clint said, "protect you, or find out who's behind these attempts."

"It's not the same thing?"

"No, it's not," Clint said. "While I'm trying to find out who's behind the sabotage and attempt on your life, somebody could still kill you. If I'm charged with protecting you, keeping you alive, there's no way I can find out who's behind it all."

"I see," she said. "What was it Delilah thought you should do?"

"Just speak to you," he said, "and see what you wanted."

"You mean she wasn't specific?"

"She just thought you needed help."

"Maybe we should call her back in and ask her what she thinks you should do."

"I tell you what," Clint said, standing up. "You think it over and let me know what you decide." He walked to the door. "If you decide you want my help, you can tell me what you want me to do, and then I'll decide if I want to do it."

"No, wait," she said, before he could leave. "I know I like to be independent and do things for myself, but maybe this isn't the time for that. Please, sit."

He sat back down.

"Delilah is probably right," she said. "You're certainly the man to help me. You've dealt with killers before."

"Once or twice," he said.

"Tell me what I need to do."

"You need to hire some men for security," Clint said. "Put them in your casino, your theater, your dining room, even in the alleys around your building. You need to be sure that if anyone causes trouble they can immediately be dealt with. And that nobody has the opportunity to start a fire."

"Are you going to tell me I need a bodyguard."

"Until this is all dealt with, yes," Clint said. "And I think I have just the man."

"You?"

"No, not me," Clint said. "He's on your front door."

"Roy?"

"Do you know who Roy once was?" he asked.

"No."

"He was a talented heavyweight fighter name Honey Roy DuPre."

"I need a fighter?"

"You need a tough man by your side wherever you go."

"Why not you?"

"Because if I agree to get actively involved, I want to find out who's behind all this. Who wants to put you out of business?"

"Every other theater and casino owner in San Francisco," she said.

"Well, I think that's going a little overboard," Clint said. "Most professional men—and women—understand that in business you have competitors. They don't all try to burn them out."

"So how will you find out who it is?"

"By asking questions," Clint said. "For instance, who have you had trouble with, personally?"

"There's a few."

"Write them all down," Clint said. "And have you spoken with the police, at all?"

"Just last night, when we had the fires," she said. "There were a couple of policemen here."

"You need to talk to a detective," Clint said. "San Francisco's got a very modern police department. You need to make use of them."

"I don't really get along with policemen," she said. "In the past, with other businesses in other towns, I've been closed down."

"Are you doing anything here that might get you closed down?" he asked.

"No," she said, without hesitation.

"Then you probably have nothing to worry about."

"I only need to ask one more question," she said.

"What's that?"

"Will Clint Adams help me?"

Clint thought about what Duke Farrell said about him always getting involved with other people's troubles.

"I'll try."

"Where do we start?"

Chapter Fourteen

"Have Delilah bring Honey Roy up here," Clint said. "We'll see if he wants a different job."

Genevieve stood immediately and went to the door. Apparently, Delilah was right outside. She told her to go downstairs and get Roy and bring him up, then came back to her desk.

"What next?"

"I'll have to make inquiries about men who can be trusted," Clint said.

"You trust someone to make those recommendations?"

"My friend, Duke Farrell."

"I've heard of him, and his place," she said. "You don't think he's threatened by the Red Lady?"

"Not at all," Clint said. "I've known him a long time, and I trust him."

"All right. And after that?"

"The police."

"Do I have to go to the police station?"

"After last night's fires, I bet we can get someone to come here."

"And you'll be here?"

"Yes."

There was a knock on the door.

"Come in," Genevieve called.

The door opened and the hulking form of Honey Roy DuPre came in.

"Delilah says you want to see me, Ma'am."

"Yes, Roy, come in. Mr. Adams and I want to ask you a question."

He came into the room and closed the door behind him. Once again, Delilah was left on the outside.

"Mr. Adams feels I need a bodyguard, and that you're the man for the job. That is, if you want it."

"At double the pay you're getting now," Clint added.

Genevieve looked surprised, but recovered quickly and said, "Yes, double."

"And what do I have to do, exactly?" Honey asked.

"You go everywhere she goes and keep her safe."

"Everywhere?" he asked.

"Within reason," she said.

"Yes," Clint said, "there'll be certain times you'll be standing in front of a door, when you can't go inside."

"Do I need to carry a weapon?"

"I think that would be wise, Roy," Clint said. "Do you have a problem with guns?"

"No, Sir."

"Do you have a gun?"

"Yes, Sir."

"On you?"

"No, I don't carry it."

"You'll have to start," Clint said. "And I want to see it. You'll be starting your new job tomorrow, so bring it with you."

"Yes, Sir."

"And you don't have to call me sir. Just call me Clint."

"Yes, s—all right, Clint. Um, is this because of the fires last night?"

"And other things," Clint said. "You'll be filled in on everything tomorrow by Miss Genevieve."

"Genevieve?"

"That's me," Genevieve said.

"Oh," Honey said. "I just always think of you as the Red Lady."

"Miss Genevieve will do fine," Clint said.

"Yes, si—uh, right, Clint."

"You can finish up on the door today," Clint said. "In fact, I'll probably want to talk to you on the way out."

"Okay," Honey Roy said, and left.

"I think I'll feel safe with him," Genevieve said. "He really fills a room."

"He does that." Clint stood.

"Are you leaving?"

"I'm going to talk to Duke and see if I can get a police detective to meet us here tomorrow."

"I'll need a new doorman."

"I'll bet Honey Roy can recommend somebody," Clint said. "I was going to talk to him on the way out, anyway. I'll ask."

"Thank you," she said. "And thank you for agreeing to help."

"Thank Delilah," Clint said. "She got me interested."

"I'll do that."

"See you in the morning, Genevieve."

"I'll arrange for breakfast," she said.

"That's fine."

"In fact," she went on, "I can put you in a room, here."

"That might be a good idea," Clint said. "I'll bring my belongings, but I'll leave my horse at Duke's." He headed for the door. "I'll see you in the morning."

As he opened the door and stepped out, he saw Delilah waiting there.

"Well?" she asked.

"She's asked for my help."

"I knew she would!" Delilah said, happily.

"I told her I'm doing it for you."

Delilah looked surprised.

"How did she take that?"

"She took it well," Clint said. "You won't be fired."

"She'd never dare."

"Why not?"

Delilah waved her hand.

"Never mind. Where are you off to now?"

"I'm going to talk to Honey Roy, and then try to find some men for security."

"Where?"

"I'll ask my friend Duke to recommend some."

"Off you go, then," Delilah said. "I have to talk with Genevieve."

"I'll see you both tomorrow morning," he said, and headed down the hallway.

***

Delilah knocked and entered.

"You played it just right," she said. "He's in."

"That's good," Genevieve said. "I'm not looking forward to being killed. That big brute will keep me safe."

Delilah sat in the chair Clint had occupied.

"I'll have a drink," she said to Genevieve.

"Right away," Genevieve said, and hurried to the sideboard to pour some wine.

Chapter Fifteen

At the door Clint stopped to speak with Honey Roy.

"Thanks for the job," Honey said to him. "And the pay raise."

"Just keep her safe from harm," Clint said.

"I'll try."

"I need something else."

"What is it?"

"A new doorman," Clint said. "Do you have a friend that will do?"

"I have several."

"Ex-fighters?"

"One."

"Offer him the job, same pay you were getting. Will he take it?"

"He will."

"Good. Have him here tomorrow morning. And don't forget to bring your gun."

"I won't."

"See you then."

Clint left and headed for Duke's.

***

"Of course I'll keep your horse here," Duke said. "And your room is here whenever you want it back."

"Thanks, Duke."

They were sitting at Duke's table in the saloon.

"I need one other thing," Clint said. "Actually, several other things."

"Like what?"

"Men who will work security for the Red Lady."

"Ah," Duke said, "I assume you mean reliable, trustworthy men."

"I do."

"How many?"

"I think six to start with," Clint said. "All good hands with a gun. Do you know that many?"

"I think I do," Duke said. "How fast do you need 'em?"

"As fast as you can get them."

"I'll need tomorrow to recruit them," Duke said. "Day after?"

"Good enough."

Duke waved the bartender over with two fresh beers.

"One other thing," Clint said.

"What's that?"

"Don't say 'I told you so.' "

Duke raised his mug and said, "I swear."

***

Clint's next move was the police department. He presented himself to the building on Mission Street and asked to see a detective. A uniformed policeman brought a man in his thirties, wearing a suit.

"Can we go to your office?" Clint asked.

"I'm a detective," the man said, "not a lieutenant or captain. I have no office. We can talk here."

They sat on a bench.

"I'm Detective Jim Muldoon," the man said.

"Clint Adams is my name."

"The Gunsmith?"

"That's right."

"What are you doing in San Francisco?"

"I came here to drink and gamble," Clint said, "but I've gotten involved in something else."

"What else?"

Clint explained about the fires at the Red Lady, and the other incidents, including Genevieve almost being run down.

"What do you want from us?" the man asked.

"An investigation," Clint said.

"Into what?"

"The fires, the other acts of sabotage," Clint said. "And the attempt on her life."

"That sounds like it could have been an accident," Muldoon said.

"The fires, then," Clint said. "Obviously they were set. If we find out by whose order, we might find out who's behind all these attempts."

"I'll have to talk to my boss," Muldoon said. "If he okays it, I'll come and talk to her."

"Soon, I hope."

"Like I said, if he okays it, I can come out tomorrow."

"Fine."

"And will you be there when I arrive?"

"I will."

"So you're working for her?"

"I'm not getting paid," Clint said. "I'm just trying to help."

"All right, then."

They stood and shook hands.

"I hope I get the okay," Muldoon said, "I've been wanting to see that place."

"Oh, you'll see it." Clint promised. "The whole operation."

He bid the man goodbye and left, hoping he would see him again.

Chapter Sixteen

Clint would have gambled that night—probably poker with Ben Silver—but instead he stayed in Duke's that afternoon and evening. Later he went to his room to pack his things for a move to the Red Lady. That done, he went downstairs for dinner. He ate in the dining room alone and ordered a steak.

After eating, he went into Duke's casino for a bit of poker before turning in. It didn't seem he'd get to play as much as he was looking forward to, unless he got in a few hands at the Red Lady.

The next morning, he rose and took a cab to the Red Lady. He found Honey Roy at the door with another, smaller man.

"Good morning, Roy," Clint said.

"Clint," Honey said. "This is Leo Carey. He was a good middleweight in his time."

Clint looked at the man, who seemed to be in his fifties.

"Does he understand his job?" Clint asked.

"I do, Sir," Leo said. "No one gets in without approval."

"Right." Clint looked at Honey Roy. "Come inside with me."

In the lobby, Clint turned to Honey Roy.

"Let me see your gun."

Honey took it from his pocket, with difficulty. It was a big, old Navy Colt.

"My God," Clint said, "that will blow up in your hand the first time you try to use it."

"It's all I have."

Clint was wearing his Peacemaker in his holster and had his New Line in his belt. He wouldn't give up his own Colt and the New Line was too small for Honey's hand.

"I'll get you something else," Clint said. "For now, keep that in your pocket."

"All right."

"Come with me."

Clint knew the way through the halls to Genevieve's office. When he got there, he knocked and entered. Both Genevieve and Delilah were there, wearing their red and purple.

"Good morning," Genevieve said. "I'm glad you're here. I'm starving for breakfast."

"So am I."

"Delilah will join us," Genevieve said, as both women stood. "We'll go to the dining room."

"Fine."

"And will Roy join us?" she asked.

"He'll stand by and watch for trouble."

"There won't be any trouble in our dining room," Genevieve said.

"You never know," Clint said.

The four of them left the office and walked to the dining room, where a table set for four was waiting. They were the only ones there.

"Roy has to have breakfast," Genevieve said.

"He can sit at a table by the door, where he can keep watch."

Genevieve turned to the waiter.

"Bring Roy whatever he wants."

"Yes, Ma'am."

"Thank you, Miss Genevieve," Roy said, and followed the waiter to another table.

Clint and the ladies sat, and two waiters brought out platters of eggs, ham, and potatoes, and baskets of biscuits.

"Is this enough food?" Genevieve asked.

"It's plenty," Clint said.

As they ate, Delilah asked, "What's happening with security, and the police?"

"With any luck they'll all be here tomorrow."

"What about today?"

"Today we'll have to make do with Honey Roy and me for security," Clint said. "If that suits you ladies."

"It suits us fine," Genevieve said, "Just fine."

Chapter Seventeen

Over breakfast Clint explained that Duke was recruiting security men, and Detective Muldoon was looking for permission to investigate.

"So we won't know anything til tomorrow?" Genevieve asked.

"That's right," Clint said. "Today you have me, Honey Roy, and his friend, Leo, at the door."

"Leo?" Delilah asked.

"Another ex-fighter," Clint said. "He'll handle the door."

"So what do we do in the meantime?" Genevieve asked.

"Open for business, as usual," Clint said. "You'll stay inside for the whole day. Honey Roy will stay by your side. I'll keep a sharp eye out for trouble."

"You won't leave the premises?" Genevieve asked.

"None of us will," Clint said. "Not til tomorrow."

"After breakfast I'll show you to your room," Delilah said.

"Good," Clint said. "After that you can show me around again, this time showing me everything."

"Everything?" she asked.

"Whatever you didn't show me yesterday."

"Oh," she said, "everything."

***

After breakfast Genevieve went back to her office, with Honey Roy by her side. Delilah showed Clint to a room.

"Is this good enough?" she asked.

It was small, but very clean, with only a bed and an end table.

"It's fine," Clint said.

"I doubt you'll be spending very much time in here," she said.

"Why's that?"

"It's only a few doors down from mine," she said.

"Delilah," he said, "we're not going to have very much time for that."

"But we have time for this." She put her arms around his neck, pulled him down to her and kissed him.

"Just enough time," he agreed, kissing her back. "But that's all."

She frowned but released him.

"Time to show me around," he said.

"Remind me," she said, "exactly what do you want me to show you?"

"I told you," he said. "Whatever you didn't show me yesterday. Other entrances, back doors, the way to the roof, is there a basement? Everything."

"Then we better get started," she said. "There's a lot to see."

***

Delilah took a good part of the day to show Clint all he wanted to see. By the time they were done, he knew every entry and egress. By dinner time they took the meal with Genevieve. This time the dining room had many other diners, but Honey Roy still sat at a table by the door.

"So how did you and Honey Roy get along today?" Clint asked.

"He's very respectful," Genevieve said. "But we talked very little."

"Talking isn't part of his job," Clint said. "He's to protect you."

"Then he's done his job nicely, so far," she said.

"Good."

Two waiters came and cleared the table, then brought pie and coffee.

"What will you do tonight?" Genevieve asked.

"I think I'll spend time in your casino," Clint said. "But first I'll make sure things are going smoothly in your theater, and here in your dining room."

"And I'll be in my office," Genevieve said. "With Honey Roy."

"Good," Clint said. He wiped his mouth and stood. "I'll be making regular rounds, so I might as well start today."

"Would you like me to come with you?" Delilah asked.

"That's not necessary," Clint said. "I know my way around now. I'll see you later."

He walked to the door and stopped at Honey Roy's table.

"Clint."

"Yes?"

"Am I supposed to keep her alive," Honey asked, "*and* do as she says?"

"That's right, Honey Roy," Clint answered, "do whatever she says. She's the one paying you."

"Just checking," Honey Roy said.

Clint left the dining room to make his rounds.

***

Genevieve entered her office, with Honey Roy behind her.

"Make sure that door is locked," she told him.

"Yes, Ma'am."

He locked the door and turned to face her. She leaned back against her desk and smiled.

"Now let me see those trousers hit the floor."

"Yes, Ma'am."

Honey Roy undid his trousers, letting them fall around his ankles.

"Oh my," Genevieve said, when she saw his huge cock. "It's not even hard and it's that big?"

"I guess so."

"We'll have to do something about that."

She straightened, undid her red gown and let it drop to the floor. Honey Roy took in the sight of her long, lean body, with small teacup breasts, and slender hips. The bush of hair between her legs was as red as the hair on her beautiful head.

His cock began to swell.

"Ah," she said, "that's more like it."

She walked to him, got down on her knees and took his cock in her hands, stroking it until it was standing straight and tall. Then she opened her mouth and pushed the large, swollen head between her lips, wetting it thoroughly. She stood then, walked to her desk and, with a swipe of her arm, cleared it, and sat on it.

"Come here," she said.

"Uh, my boots—"

"Shuffle over here," she told him.

He did so.

She settled back on the desk and spread her legs. He stepped forward to press the head of his cock to her pussy.

"Not yet," she said, as if speaking to a child. "I want your face between my legs."

"What?"

She pointed to her vagina.

"Your face," she said, "and get your tongue busy."

He fell to his knees, pressed his face to her fragrant pussy, and did as she told him.

It was his job.

Chapter Eighteen

Clint finished his rounds and entered the casino. He found Delilah already there.

"I've been waiting for you," she said.

"Did you think I'd get lost?" he asked.

"No," she said. "I just missed you."

"Well," Clint said, "it was necessary for me to check all the doors and rooms."

"You saved the casino for last," she said. "Are you going to gamble?"

"That wouldn't be a good idea," Clint said. "I can't afford to be distracted."

"Of course not," she said. "Not by anything."

"Where's Genevieve?" he asked.

"In her office, I suppose," Delilah said, "with Honey Roy."

"Good," he said. "If she's there, she's safe. And you should be somewhere safe."

"Like in my room?" she asked. "Locked away? I think I'll be safe inside these walls."

"Maybe I should get you your own bodyguard, as well."

"That could be you."

"I'm going to be pretty busy," he told her.

"Maybe I could come with you." she said. "That way you'll always know where I am, and that I'm safe."

"I'm going to be outside, where it's dangerous. You'll have security if you stay inside."

"When whoever's trying to ruin us finds out that you're helping, what do you think they'll do?"

"They'll either quit, or try to kill me, too."

"So who's going to watch your back?"

"I'm working on that, too," Clint said. "I'm going to go and check with my friend, Duke, and see what he's been able to do for us."

"You better come back safe," she said, "or I'll feel real bad I brought you into this."

"I'll be back," he said.

"Let me know when you are."

He promised he would and headed for the front door.

***

He stopped just outside to talk with Leo.

"No trouble, Mr. Adams," the fighter said. "Nobody tryin' to get in with guns."

"Good," Clint said, "let's hope it stays that way."

He waved down a cab in front of the building and told the driver to take him to Duke's in Portsmouth Square.

***

He found Duke walking the floor in the casino and to his office.

"I've got six men coming to the Red Lady tomorrow morning at nine a.m.," Duke told him. "They'll be meeting you out front."

"That's fine."

"Did you talk to the police?" Duke asked.

"A Detective Muldoon. He's going to see what he can do after he checks with his boss."

"I've heard of him. What are you gonna do while he's checking?"

"Try and find out who's behind this whole mess," Clint told him. "I was hoping you could help me with some likely names. Casino owners who'd feel threatened by The Red Lady."

"I doubt anyone from the Portsmouth Square houses cares what she's doing on the Barbary Coast. But I can give you some names from down there."

"That'll do."

"And while you're nosing around," Duke asked, "who's gonna be watching your back?"

"Now there's something I thought you could help me with, too."

"I think I have somebody in mind," Duke said, thoughtfully. "I'll try to get ahold of him and get him over to the Red Lady tomorrow."

"Okay," Clint said, "I appreciate it."

"How are you getting along with the Red Lady herself?" Duke asked.

"She's doing pretty much what I tell her to do, for now," Clint said. "The key was getting her to realize she needed help."

"As far as she's concerned," Duke said, "you came to San Francisco at just the right time."

"This isn't what I was expecting when I came here," Clint admitted.

"Well, maybe you can get this put to rest in time to still have some time to relax."

"I hope so," Clint said. "I really was looking forward to relaxing."

Chapter Nineteen

Back at the Red Lady, Delilah entered Genevieve's office. Honey Roy was seated in a chair near the door. Everything Genevieve had swept from the desk had been replaced, and she sat behind it, in her red gown. A look passed between her and the bodyguard, which did not escape Delilah.

"Honey Roy, could you step into the hall, please?" Delilah asked.

"I'm supposed to stay with Miss Genevieve at all times," the big man said.

"She's in no danger from me," Delilah said.

"Go ahead, Roy," Genevieve said. "I'll be fine."

Reluctantly, Honey Roy stepped from the room and Delilah closed the door.

"He wasn't put in here with you so you could fuck him!" Delilah hissed.

"Please," Genevieve said. "He has a massive cock. How could I not?"

"You made the decision before you saw his cock."

"I could see it outlined against his trousers," Genevieve said. "Besides, tell me you haven't fucked the Gunsmith."

"That's my business," Delilah said.

"And fucking Honey Roy is mine."

"But your business *is* my business," Delilah said. "Everything you do is my business, because everybody thinks you are me."

"I agreed to act as The Red Lady for you," Genevieve said, "but that was before I knew somebody was going to try to kill you. So forgive me for wanting a little pleasure before I die."

"You're not going to die," Delilah said. "Clint won't allow it."

"You really think he can stop it?"

"If anyone can find out who's behind all this, and stop it, he can."

"A drink?" Genevieve asked.

Delilah sank into the chair across from the desk.

"Yes."

Genevieve poured two glasses of wine and gave one to Delilah.

"Here's to Clint putting an end to all of this," she said, raising her glass.

"Amen," Delilah said. She drank her wine and stood up. "I'll send your bodyguard back in."

"Do that," Genevieve said, sitting behind the desk.

But as Delilah started for the door Genevieve asked, "When will you come out from under your purple dresses and let it be known you are the Red Lady?"

"Soon," she said. "As soon as my success is assured."

"Don't you think this place is successful?" Genevieve asked.

"I want to be successful," Delilah said, "and safe."

She went out the door and sent Honey Roy back in.

***

Clint spent most of the night walking the halls, checking doors, even after business hours were over and all the venues were closed. Honey Roy was sitting in a chair outside Genevieve's room. They nodded to each other as Clint walked by, finally on his way to his own quarters. He also walked past Delilah's door but made no attempt to enter. Not while Honey Roy was seated in the hall.

When he got to his own room and entered, however, he found Delilah already in his bed.

"You shouldn't be in here," he told her.

"I came in before Honey Roy sat outside Genevieve's door. Besides, she knows about us."

"She does?"

"Of course," Delilah said, "just as I know she's fucking Roy."

"What?"

"Well," she said, "you told him to do whatever she wanted."

"I didn't mean that," he said. "He can make up his own mind about that."

"And you think he'd refuse her?"

"Well . . . no."

"Then come here," she said, tossing the sheet back to show that she was completely nude. "That is, unless you want to refuse me."

He studied her full breasts and hips, pale skin, luminous eyes and beautiful smile and said, "No, of course not."

"Good." She extended her arms. "Then come to me."

He walked to the bed, removed his gunbelt, hung it on the bedpost, and proceeded to disrobe. When he was completely naked, she took hold of his cock and stroked it. When it was fully hard, she tugged on him until he joined her in the bed. She pushed him onto his back and shimmied down so that she was lying between his legs.

"Besides," she said, "where am I safer than right here?"

He was about to answer, but when she engulfed him with her wet, hot mouth, it took his breath away.

Chapter Twenty

Clint was coming down the stairs the next morning when he saw Leo in the lobby. Delilah was still asleep in his bed, and Honey Roy was still seated outside Genevieve's door.

When Leo spotted Clint, he waved frantically.

"What's up, Leo?"

"Some men out front wanna see you, Mr. Adams. They say Duke Farrell sent them."

"Okay," Clint said, "let's see what they want."

He went to the front door with Leo and stepped outside. Six men were waiting there, and one of them came up the steps.

"Mr. Adams?" the man asked.

"That's right."

"Duke Farrell sent us over," the man said. "Something about you needing a security force."

"That's right."

"Well," the man said, "we're your men."

"What's your name?"

"I'm Todd Folsom." He quickly reeled off the names of the other five men. They all appeared to be in their thirties, some short, some tall, all dressed cleanly. He saw they were armed, Folsom with two guns, one on his hip, another in a shoulder holster.

"Why don't you come in," Clint said. "The others can wait outside a bit longer."

Folsom turned to the others and waved a placating hand, then followed Clint inside.

"We can talk over breakfast," Clint said.

"I've had breakfast," Folsom said.

"Well, I'm hungry. Come and sit with me."

He led Folsom to the dining room, which was not yet open for the day. Clint sat and told the waiter to bring ham-and-eggs and coffee, two cups. When the coffee arrived, he poured some for Folsom.

"Do you speak for the other men?" Clint asked.

"I do."

"Then tell me their backgrounds, and yours."

Folsom quickly went through each man's qualifications, and then his own. He had been a soldier for seven years. Since then, he had been for hire, as were the others.

"Guns for hire?" Clint asked.

"Not for anything illegal," Folsom said.

"I'm not worried about that," Clint said. "Can you all use a gun?"

"We can."

"All right, then," Clint said. "Let's talk price."

***

They agreed on a price and Folsom brought the other men into the dining room. They all had ham-and-eggs—including Folsom—while Clint explained the job. Two of them would be stationed on the back doors. One each would be stationed in the casino, theater and dining room. Folsom would roam from station to station. And if there was any trouble, they would all rally to it.

"What if there's trouble in more than one room?" one man asked.

"I doubt that many armed men would get past the door," Clint said, "but if there is, you'll split into two groups. And don't worry, I'll be right there with you."

"That's a comfort," another man said, "considering who you are."

"You'll all report to Folsom every morning, to see if there's a change in station."

"When do we start?" Folsom asked.

"Right after breakfast."

After that, they all bent to the task of eating. When they were done they left the dining room to go to their stations.

"Folsom!" Clint snapped

"Sir?"

"Do you have other guns at home?"

"I do."

"Let me see that one," he said, pointing to the other in the shoulder holster.

Folsom took it out and handed it to Clint. It was a Colt Paterson, not large, but big enough.

"I'd like to take this one," Clint said. "Can you replace it?"

"Easily. It's yours."

"Thank you."

Folsom nodded and left the room. Several minutes later, while Clint sat over another cup of coffee, Delilah and Genevieve entered, accompanied by Honey Roy. The women joined Clint at his table, while Honey Roy sat at a table by the door.

"If you ladies will excuse me," he said, standing.

"You're not staying?" Delilah asked.

"I have things to do," Clint said. "I'm hoping the detective from the police department will be arriving."

He walked to the door, stopped at Honey Roy's table.

"This is for you," he said, handing him the Colt.

"Thanks," the ex-fighter said. "What do I do with the other one?"

"Throw it away," Clint said. "The Colt Paterson will do until I find something else for you."

"Thanks," Roy said again.

Clint returned to the lobby and opened the front door.

"Leo."

"Yes, sir?"

"I'm expecting a policeman this morning," Clint said. "When he arrives, find me immediately."

"A policeman?"

"Is that a problem?"

"Um, I don't get along good with lawmen."

"All you have to do is ask him to wait, and then fetch me."

"Okay," Leo said, nodding, "I guess I can do that."

Chapter Twenty-One

It didn't take long for Leo to come looking for Clint. He found him standing outside the casino entrance.

"A Detective Muldoon is at the front door," the ex-fighter told him.

"Okay, let him in, Leo," Clint said.

Clint was waiting in the lobby when the detective came through the door. They shook hands.

"Good to see you, Detective," Clint said.

"My chief decided the Red Lady deserved some investigation," the man said. "Can I talk to her?"

"Of course," Clint said. "She's in her office. I'll take the long way and show you around."

By the time they got to Genevieve's door, the detective had seen most of the operation.

"This place is very impressive," he said. "No wonder somebody wants to burn it down. Most of the Barbary Coast places won't be able to compete."

"So one of them is trying to close her down or kill her," Clint said.

"We'll see."

Clint knocked on Genevieve's door. It was opened by Honey Roy.

"Clint," the big man said. "Who's this?"

"Detective Muldoon," Clint said. "He's here to see the Red Lady. Detective, this is Honey Roy DuPre."

"The fighter?" Muldoon asked. "I saw you fight. You should've been champ."

"Thanks," Honey Roy said, "I think so, too. Miss Genevieve is waiting."

"Is she as beautiful as they say?" Muldoon asked.

"More," Honey Roy said. "Come in."

Muldoon looked at Clint.

"Are you coming?"

"It's your investigation."

"So it is."

Muldoon stepped through the door and Honey Roy closed it.

So the investigation was started, and the security force was in place. Now all Clint needed was Duke's recommendation for someone to watch his back as he launched his own investigation.

***

"You're Irish?" Genevieve asked Muldoon.

"I am."

"You don't sound Irish."

"I trained myself to not have an accent," the man said. "It's bad enough I have an Irish name."

"Has it held you back?" she asked.

"It has," Muldoon said. "I'd be a Lieutenant otherwise."

"Well," she said, "maybe if you solve this problem of mine, you'll be made a Lieutenant."

"It could be," Muldoon said.

"You're a good-looking man. Are you married?"

"I am," Muldoon said. "I have two children."

"That's a pity."

"What?"

"Nothing," she said. "Never mind. Please, ask your questions . . .

***

Clint left the Red Lady and told Leo he would be back.

He found Duke in his office.

"I have your man," Duke said. "He's an ex-Pinkerton, gone out on his own."

"I could've gotten Tal Roper or John Locke, but there's no time, so I'll have to depend on your man. Who is he?"

"The man's name is Augustus Hardcastle."

"I know that name," Clint said. "He worked for Pink-
erton during the war."

"Did you work with him?"

"No," Clint said, "we were sent separate ways."

"He's due here any minute," Duke said. "If you want
somebody else."

"No," Clint said, "Gus Hardcastle will be fine."

"Then have a drink with me and we'll wait for him
together."

"Sure."

Clint sat, and Duke poured two glasses of whiskey.
He gave one to Clint and sat behind his desk with the
other.

After a few moments there was a knock on the door.
One of Duke's men poked his head in.

"Gus Hardcastle's here, boss."

"Good," Duke said. "Send him in."

The man withdrew, then the door opened and another
man entered. Clint had seen Hardcastle once during the
war. This was a much older, more grizzled version of the
same man.

"Gus," Duke said, "do you know Clint Adams?"

"I know of him," Hardcastle said. "We both worked
for Old Allan durin' the war."

Clint stood and the two men shook hands.

"Duke tells me you need help."

"I need someone to watch my back while I'm looking for the man who wants the Red Lady dead."

"The place, or the woman?" Hardcastle asked.

"Both. That's why I need somebody I can trust to watch my back," Clint said.

"What makes you think you can trust me?"

"Duke says so," Clint said. "And you had a good reputation during the war."

"That was a long time ago."

"Are you saying I can't trust you?"

"Oh, you can," Hardcastle said. "I'm just sayin' neither of us is the man we were then. Those men were . . ." Clint read the look on his face.

". . . younger?" Clint asked.

Hardcastle laughed.

"Oh yeah, we were younger," he said. "What do you want me to do?"

"Go where I go and watch my back."

"And do I get paid?"

"Yes," Clint said, "by The Red Lady."

"Ah," Hardcastle said, "then count me in."

Chapter Twenty-Two

Gus Hardcastle returned to the Red Lady, with Clint. He was introduced to Leo, as they entered. Once inside Clint introduced him to Folsom and the security force, then took him to Genevieve's office to meet Honey Roy and the Red Lady.

"Mr. Hardcastle," Genevieve said, standing behind her desk, "it's a pleasure."

"It's my pleasure, Ma'am," Hardcastle said. "You're even more beautiful than I heard."

"I thought you were here to watch Clint's back," she said, "not to be so charming."

"I can be real charmin' when I'm bein' paid well," he told her.

"I'm sure Clint told you you're being paid *very* well," she replied.

"He did."

"And so I guess we better get to it," Clint said.

"Let me know how it goes," she said, as they left.

"Now what?" Hardcastle asked.

"Duke gave me a few names," Clint said, "people who run Barbary Coast casinos who might not be happy with the Red Lady's success."

"What if Duke's just sending you after people he don't like?" Hardcastle asked.

"I trust he wouldn't do that," Clint said.

"Then I'm with you," Hardcastle said. "Who's first?"

"Duke says a place called The Shanghai Palace has been hit hard by the Red Lady's success."

"I know that place," Hardcastle said. "It's kind of rough. I wouldn't think it catered to the same crowd."

"Duke said it's run by a man named Albrecht Muller."

"He's known as Bert Muller," Hardcastle said.

"Have you met him?"

"No, I've just heard of him. He has a reputation for not being a pleasant man."

"Well, why don't we go and find out," Clint said. "According to Duke it's walking distance from here."

"Then let's walk," Hardcastle said.

***

The Shanghai Palace was only a couple of blocks from the docks. As they entered, it looked like a lot of the clientele were sailors, and dock workers.

"Let's get a couple of beers at the bar and look around," Clint said.

"Suits me."

The Palace wasn't very busy, but that could have been because of the early hour, and not The Red Lady taking their business.

"Two beers," Clint told the weary looking bartender.

"Comin' up."

With their beers in hand, they turned their backs to the bar and cast their eyes upon the activities in the place. Many of the gaming tables were dormant, at the moment.

"It's a little dead in here," Clint said to the bartender.

"It'll pick up," the man said.

"I heard something about The Red Lady taking your business."

"That place?" The bartender made a rude noise with his mouth. "That's too damn hoity toity for our customers. No, our people keep comin' here. If you stay around long enough, you'll see."

"Is the owner around?"

"Mr. Muller?" the bartender said. "He comes round in the evenings."

The bartender moved off down the bar.

"Whataya think?" Hardcastle asked.

"What else would he say?"

"Are we gonna stay and wait?"

"Let's finish these beers and move on," Clint said. "We'll come back later."

They downed their beers and left.

***

The next place was on the docks. Rather than a casino, it was simply a saloon with gaming tables. Clint didn't see how it could ever be competition for the Red Lady, or vice versa. It was called The Rust Bucket Saloon.

"Who owns this place?" Clint asked, as they stood in front of it. "Duke didn't say."

"His name's Jack Finley," Hardcastle said.

"Do you know him?"

"I've met him a time or two when I gambled here," Hardcastle said.

"What's he like?"

"Not a very ambitious sort," Hardcastle said. "He's happy with this place as it is."

"And if he felt it was being threatened?"

"He wouldn't hesitate to kill to keep it."

"Then we better talk to him."

They went through the batwing doors.

Chapter Twenty-Three

They went to the bar, and Hardcastle stopped Clint before he ordered.

"No clean glasses," he said. "Let's get bottles."

"Right." Clint looked at the bartender. "Two bottles of beer."

The man nodded.

Even at an early hour the tables were busy. As with the Shanghai, the customers were dockworkers and sailors. And they probably did shanghai men from here.

The bartender put two bottles of beer on the bar.

"Is Mr. Finley here?" Clint asked.

"The back room."

"His office?"

"What office?" the bartender said. "He's in the back room, behind the curtain."

Clint and Hardcastle took their bottles and crossed the room to the curtain. When they pulled it back a man looked up from the stack of bills he was counting out on the table in front of him. He was a wizened sixty, squat and thin.

"If you're here to rob me you won't make it out the door," the man rasped.

"Finley?" Clint asked.

"That's right. Who are you?"

"Clint Adams. This is Hardcastle."

Finley stared at them a moment.

"Hardcastle," he said. "I know you." He looked at Clint. "What's the Gunsmith doin' here? This place is beneath you."

"That's right," Clint said. "I'm here on behalf of The Red Lady."

"That place!" Finley sat back in his chair. "What does that woman want with me?"

"She wants to know if you're behind somebody setting fire to her place," Clint said. "And trying to kill her on the street by running her down."

"Really?" Finley said, smiling. "Well, tell your good lady that if I wanted her burned out, she'd be burned out. And if I wanted her dead, she'd be dead."

"That's bold talk," Clint said.

"To the Gunsmith, yes," Finley said. "If I lie to you, you'll kill me. I know your reputation."

"So you had nothing to do with either act," Clint said. "Or any other."

"Nothing."

"Then who do you think might be behind it all?" Clint asked.

"That's an interestin' question."

"Give me an interesting answer," Clint said. "One that'll stop me from looking at you."

"Shanghai Palace."

"We've been there and we're going back," Clint said. "Who else?"

"The Barbary Queen," Finley said. "Run by the Slade brothers."

"Which one of them gives the orders?"

"They both do."

"Which is the oldest?"

"They're twins," Finley said. "Dolph and Danny."

"Who else?"

"Have you looked at the Portsmouth Square clubs?" the man asked.

"I haven't," Clint said. "I don't think she competes with them, yet."

"It's the 'yet' you have to look at," Finley said. "What about Duke Farrell?"

"Not a chance."

"Then that's all I got," Finley said. "If it's all right with you, I have work to do."

"Thanks for your time," Clint said.

"You're welcome."

Before stepping through the curtain Clint added, "You better hope I have no reason to come back here."

When Clint was gone Jack Finley heaved a sigh of relief, and stared down at his shaking hands.

Chapter Twenty-Four

The Barbary Queen had water from the docks flowing beneath it. That made it a perfect place to shanghai men for long sea cruises, usually to the Orient. And they would be on that boat until it returned months, sometimes years later.

It was cleaner than the Rust Bucket, larger than both the Bucket and Shanghai Palace. As Clint and Hardcastle entered, they saw few places at the bar or tables.

"It's gettin' later in the afternoon," Hardcastle pointed out. "After this we can go back to the Shanghai Palace to see Muller.

They went to the bar and elbowed some room for themselves. A couple of dockworkers looked as if they would like to protest, but noticed Clint and Hardcastle's guns and moved.

"Two beers," Clint said to the bartender, "in bottles."

Wordlessly, the bartender put two bottles on the bar.

"Hey!" Clint snapped, as the man began to move away.

"Yeah?"

"Are the Slade brothers here?"

"Who wants to know?"

Clint gave the man a hard stare and said, "I do."

"They're in their office," the barman said.

"Which one?"

"Both," the man said. "You want one, you get the other."

"Where's the office?"

"Against the back wall."

"Thanks."

Clint and Hardcastle took their bottles and headed away.

"Hey!" the bartender yelled.

"What?" Clint asked.

"Be nice and knock, huh?"

When they reached the door, they knocked.

"Yeah?"

They opened the door and stepped in. Two men in white suits looked at them. They were virtually identical, except for a scar on the face of one.

"Who're you and whataya want?" the scarred one asked.

"I'm Clint Adams, this is Gus Hardcastle."

The brothers exchanged a glance.

"What's the Gunsmith doin' in our place?" the other one asked.

"You're the Slade brothers, right?"

"Right," the scar-faced one said. "I'm Dolph."

"I'm Danny."

"Now that we're all introduced," Dolph said, "whataya want?"

"I'm looking into some trouble The Red Lady's having."

"What trouble?"

"You must've heard about the fires."

"Somebody got careless," Danny said.

"Somebody set those fires," Clint said. "I want to know who."

"So why're you here?" Dolph asked.

"You don't think we had those fires set?" Danny said.

"You must be losing some customers to the Lady," Clint said.

"I don't think so," Dolph said.

"We've got loyal customers," Danny said. "We don't need to do anything to The Red Lady."

"Somebody tried to run her down in the street," Hardcastle said. "Whataya know about that?"

"Whoa!" Dolph said. "You're accusin' us of tryin' to kill her?"

"You're crazy," Danny said. "We don't need to kill anybody."

"You see the business we're doin' out there," Dolph pointed out.

"Okay," Clint said, "give me a guess. Who do you think is suffering because of The Red Lady?"

"Nobody on the Barbary Coast," Danny said. "We've all got regular customers."

"Why not look at some of the Portsmouth Square places?"

"They'd have the same reasons you have," Clint said. "Loyal customers."

"Then maybe somebody's got a vivid imagination," Dolph said.

"No imagination," Clint said. "Somebody's out to get her. I'm going to find out who."

"You're for sure lookin' in the wrong places then," Danny told him.

"I suggest you go and look in the right place," Dolph said. "We got nothin' more to say."

"Maybe not," Clint said, "but I hope I don't have any reason to come back here."

"Take our advice, and don't," Dolph said.

"Hardcastle," Danny said, as he and Clint turned to leave.

"Yeah?"

"We've heard of you," Dolph said. "Why are you involved in this?"

"I'm just doin' a job," Hardcastle said. "There's nothin' personal."

He followed Clint out.

Chapter Twenty-Five

Clint and Hardcastle went back to the Shanghai Palace.

"Mr. Muller in?" Clint asked, the bartender.

"Yeah, he's sittin' at his table in the back. You can't miss 'im. He's got two girls with him."

Clint and Hardcastle walked to the back, found a fortyish man with a mustache sitting with two flashy looking ladies—flashy in a cheap way.

Muller looked up as they reached his table.

"Can I do somethin' for you gentlemen?" he asked.

"We'd like to talk to you about some trouble over at The Red Lady," Clint said.

"And who would you be?"

"I'm Clint Adams, this is Gus Hardcastle."

Muller thought for a few moments, then said, "Girls, take a walk."

The girls obeyed immediately, rose and walked to the bar.

Clint and Hardcastle sat. The chairs were pleasantly warm from the girls' backsides.

"I heard there's been trouble over there," Muller said. "Anything I can do to help?"

He spoke English very formally, like someone who had learned it as a second language.

"You've got a pretty good operation, here," Clint said. "You lose any business since The Lady opened?"

"Not that I noticed."

"Really?" Clint leaned back and looked around. "It looks kind of quiet here tonight."

"It picks up on the weekend," Muller said.

"The Red Lady is full every night."

"What do you have to do with that place?" Muller asked.

"One might say I was chief of security."

"Well, there's nothing for you to do here," Muller said. "I mind my own business."

"I hope that's right," Clint said. He told the man what he had told the others. "I'd hate to have to come back here."

"Believe me," Muller said, "I would hate that as well."

***

It was dinner time when Clint and Hardcastle returned to The Red Lady.

"I'll go and get something to eat," Hardcastle said.

"No," Clint said, "you'll eat here, with me. So will the others we hired."

"The food here is libel to be too fancy for my tender stomach," Hardcastle said.

"You can order anything you want," Clint said. "The cook will make whatever you like."

"A steak would be fine," Hardcastle said.

"A steak it is, then. Come on."

When they reached the dining room, many of the tables were occupied. Sitting alone by the door was Honey Roy, who nodded to them. In the back Delilah and Genevieve were seated, and waved at Clint to join them.

"I'll sit here with Honey Roy," Hardcastle said. "We'll get to know each other better."

"Come and sit with us," Clint said.

"I don't think so," Hardcastle said. "My table manners might offend the two fine ladies."

"Gus—"

"Go," Hardcastle said, "eat. I'll be here when you need me."

Hardcastle sat with Honey Roy as Clint crossed the floor to join Delilah and Genevieve.

"It's good to see you," Genevieve said. "Your security force has been doing a fine job. They evicted several troublemakers."

"Just troublemakers?"

"Yes," Delilah said, "they were starting fights. Nothing more."

"What about you?" Genevieve asked. "How was your day?"

Clint sat.

"Let me order dinner and I'll tell you."

***

Over an excellent steak, Clint told them how his day went.

"They all denied any part," Delilah said. "Did you believe them all?"

"Not really," Clint said, "but I had no cause to call them liars to their faces."

"So now what?" Genevieve asked. "Will you talk to some of the Portsmouth Square houses?"

"I doubt any of them are behind this," Clint said. "But on the other hand, some of them might have heard something helpful."

"So then you will talk to them," Delilah said.

"Yes," Clint said, "tomorrow. We might find out something."

As they continued to eat, Genevieve told him of her conversation with Lieutenant Muldoon.

Chapter Twenty-Six

After dinner Clint and Hardcastle walked the property, satisfied that the dining room was secure with one of Folsom's men.

There was one man in the casino, one in the saloon, two patrolling the rear of the property.

When they left the casino, they ran into Folsom who was making his own rounds.

"We heard there was some trouble today," Clint said.

"Some fights broke out in the casino," Folsom said. "I had my man remove the combatants."

"So there was no danger to the property or the lady?" Clint asked.

"None."

"Good," Clint said. "Has the police detective been around today?"

"After he spoke with Genevieve in her office, he left. He hasn't been back,"

"Hopefully," Clint said, "He's conducting his own investigation. Your men seem to be doing a good job, Folsom. Thanks."

"They're doin' what they're bein' paid to do," Folsom said and continued his rounds.

Clint looked at Hardcastle.

"What did you hear from Honey Roy?"

"Well," Hardcastle said, "for one thing, the Red Lady is fucking him."

"Not the other way around?"

"He's only doin' what she tells him to do," Hardcastle said. "And apparently, it's no chore."

"I guess they're forming their own bind," Clint said. "It doesn't matter, as long as he keeps her safe. Anything else?"

"She flirted with the policeman," Hardcastle said. "But he's married, has children, and seemed able to resist her."

"Good for him," Clint said. "Where did he go after that? Does Honey know?"

"He left," Hardcastle said, "but he promised to launch an investigation."

"It doesn't seem as if he was anywhere we were before us," Clint observed.

"Maybe after us," Hardcastle said.

"And maybe," Clint said, "he has some ideas of his own. Seems to me we ought to talk to him, as well."

"I'll leave all the talkin' to you," Hardcastle said. "I don't like lawmen."

"You want to have a drink in the saloon?"

"I think I wanna turn in," Hardcastle said.

J.R. Roberts

"I'll show you where your room is," Clint said.

As they went upstairs and down the hall Hardcastle asked, "What about Folsom and the others?"

"There are rooms for them along here," Clint said. "They'll have to share."

"Won't that put a crimp in some of the Red Lady's business?" Hardcastle asked.

"What do you mean?"

"Where will the whores do their business?"

"There are no whores here."

"I thought there was a high-priced bordello on the grounds."

"No," Clint said, "no bordello."

"Oh," Hardcastle said, "my mistake."

Clint stopped.

"Here's your room."

"Yeah, okay," Hardcastle said. "Good-night."

"See you downstairs at breakfast"

Hardcastle went into his room and locked the door.

Honey Roy was not yet seated in the hall outside Genevieve's room.

When Clint entered his own room, he wasn't surprised to see Delilah there in the bed.

"You keep late hours," she said.

"I have to make sure everything's secure before I turn in," he said, removing his gunbelt and hanging it up.

"Come to bed," she said.

"I have to wash up first."

"This room doesn't have running water," she said. "I made sure your pitcher is full.

He walked to the dresser with the pitcher-and-basin on it, poured some water out. Then he unbuttoned his short, removed it, tossed it aside and began to wash, using a cloth.

Delilah got out of bed, came over, naked, took the cloth from him and began to wash his back, his shoulders.

"If you take off your boots and pants," she said, "I'd be happy to wash you down there."

"That won't be necessary," Clint said. "If you do that, we'll never finish."

She gave him the cloth and went back to the bed.

He pulled off his boots, trousers and underwear, washed himself thoroughly, dried off with a towel and then came to the bed.

"I can arrange for a real bath tomorrow," she said, running her hands over him. "If you like."

He turned toward her, took her into his arms, and said, "I'd like that fine."

Chapter Twenty-Seven

The next morning Clint met Hardcastle for breakfast before anyone else came down. Delilah was still asleep in his bed.

"Sleep okay?" he asked.

"Like a log," Hardcastle said, sitting across from him. "I don't think I've ever slept on a bed that comfortable."

The waiter came over.

" 'mornin', gents. What'll ya have this mornin'?"

Hardcastle looked at Clint.

"Just tell him what you want," Clint said.

"Steak and eggs, spuds, biscuits," Hardcastle said.

"Of course."

"And flapjacks."

The waiter looked at Clint.

"The same, except for the flapjacks."

"Yes, Sir. I'll be back with coffee."

As the waiter walked away, Hardcastle asked, "What's on our schedule today?"

"The Portsmouth Square houses."

"You don't really think someone from there is behind the attacks on The Red Lady."

"Actually, no, I don't," Clint said, "but someone from there might have heard something."

"That would be helpful," Hardcastle said.

"Yes, it would," Clint said. "I also want to compare notes with Muldoon."

"So you'll be goin' to the police station?"

"Yes."

"Do you mind if I don't go with you?"

"You can wait outside, or in a saloon," Clint said. "I don't think anyone in the police station is going to try to kill me."

"That's agreeable," Hardcastle said. "I believe there's a saloon across the street from the building."

"Then let's do that first, and then head for the Square."

"After breakfast, of course," Hardcastle said.

"Of course," Clint said. As the waiter appeared with their plates, Hardcastle said, "I think the food may be the best part of this job."

"I can't argue with that," Clint said, and they began to eat.

***

"I thought you said you didn't have an office," Clint said.

"This is the captain's office," Muldoon said, from behind the man's desk. "He's out today. Have a seat."

Clint sat across from the man.

"I was wondering how your investigation is going," he said.

"I seem to be a step behind you," Muldoon said. "Everywhere I go, you've already been there."

"And the answers you got?" Clint asked.

"No doubt the same as you."

"And what do you take away from all this?" Clint asked.

"I wouldn't put it past the Slade brothers," Muldoon said.

"And the others?"

"No need," Muldoon said. "They can't compete, and they wouldn't have the gumption. What's your next step?"

"I'm going to talk to some of the heads of the Portsmouth Square houses," Clint said. "See what they know."

"Do you really think it's one of them?"

"No," Clint said. "They've been around a long time. None of them feel threatened by The Red Lady. I just think one or more of them know who does."

"I hope you're right," Muldoon said.

"Are you going to be on my tail?" Clint asked.

"No," Muldoon said, "I'm taking another path."

"Maybe our paths will cross."

"Could be," Muldoon said. "Just remember, I'm official and you're not."

"I'll keep that in mind."

"Do that, Mr. Adams."

Clint stood and left the office.

***

He walked into the saloon across the street and saw Hardcastle sitting at a table with a beer.

"Want one?" Hardcastle asked.

"No," Clint said, sitting across from him, "too early for me."

"Never too early for me," Hardcastle said. "What did the man have to say?"

"Up to now he's been a step behind us," Clint said. "From this point on he's taking a different path."

"Then we're off to Portsmouth Square."

"Yes," Clint said. "We'll get as many in as we can today and finish up tomorrow. Hopefully, by then, we'll know something."

Hardcastle tipped his mug up and emptied it down his throat.

"Let's get movin' then."

Chapter Twenty-Eight

Clint and Hardcastle spent the morning visiting The Parker House, Sam Dennison's Exchange, and The El Dorado. They spoke not only with the owners, but with the casino managers. When they were asked who they might suspect of trying to burn The Red Lady down, only two names were mentioned—the Slade brothers.

"They're the only ones of that bunch who would have the nerve to do it," one manager said.

Clint and Hardcastle stopped for lunch at a local steakhouse.

"Do we want to keep talking to the other houses," Hardcastle asked, "or act on the information we've got."

"We have no information," Clint said. "We have opinions and suspicion."

"Even though, we should act before they try something again," Hardcastle said.

"We've got enough security at The Red Lady," Clint said. "And if the Slade's think we suspect them, perhaps they'll stop."

Hardcastle bit into a buttered roll.

"Even if they stop, they'll be back at it eventually," he said.

Clint leaned back to allow the waiter to set plates down.

"We'll keep talking to people," Clint said. "The rest of Portsmouth Square, even some of the Chinatown establishments. If the only names we come up with are the Slade brothers, we'll give them a choice: either leave San Francisco, or pay the consequences."

"And those consequences would be?"

"That'll be up to them."

***

They spent the rest of the afternoon hitting other houses. Clint was right about the casino owners there. They had been in business a long time, and all knew their place, and none accused any of the others. They all had low opinions of the Barbary Coast houses, and most agreed that the Barbary Queen was the best of a bad lot and would not appreciate the competition from The Red Lady.

Clint had expected the task of talking to the Portsmouth Square owners to take two days, but by the end of the first day they were done. They finished up at Duke Farrell's.

Over drinks at his table Clint asked, "What's your opinion of the Slade brothers?"

"Snakes," Duke said, "one worse than the other. When I gave you the list of names of Barbary Coast owners, they were at the top."

"Yes, they were."

"So what will you do now?" Duke asked.

"I'll confer with Detective Muldoon and see what he thinks."

"You could just sit back and wait for them to try again," Duke said. "You've got your security force in place."

"If I wait for that," Clint said, "somebody's going to die. I'd rather send them packing."

"Do you think they'll go?"

"I won't give them a choice."

"Okay," Duke said, "I meant, do you think they'll go willingly?"

"Not willingly," Clint said, "but they'll go."

"They'll have their own men, you know," Duke said. "This might start a war."

"If it does," Clint said, "it'll be a Barbary Coast war. You and the other houses in Portsmouth Square won't have to worry."

"I'd rather see no war, at all," Duke said.

"We'll see," Clint said. "It still might be avoided."

"You'll have to worry about who the Chinese will side with."

"Who runs Chinatown?" Clint asked. "I can talk to them first."

"You'll want to talk to Ben Fong," Duke said. "He runs everything from laundries to casinos."

"Ben Fong," Clint repeated. He looked at Hardcastle. "Do you know him?"

"I do."

"Will he meet with you?"

"I think he will."

"Then we'll talk to him tomorrow," Clint said. "Maybe we can keep him from taking sides."

"I'll set up a meet," Hardcastle said. "Wait here until I get back. I don't want you gettin' it in the back because I wasn't with you."

"I'll be here."

Hardcastle left.

"Good," Duke said, "maybe you can do a little gambling now."

"I thought you didn't want me cleaning you out at the tables," Clint said.

"I'll lose a little money if it keeps you alive, my friend."

Chapter Twenty-Nine

Clint passed the time playing blackjack while he waited for Hardcastle to return. He chose blackjack because he didn't like it much and knew he wouldn't get sucked into a good game, as if it was poker. He hated losing with twenty to a dealer's twenty-one, because it happened too often.

When Hardcastle walked into the casino Clint picked up his chips and left the table.

"Well?" he asked.

"He'll see us."

"When?"

"Tonight, at midnight."

"Midnight?"

"He's a dramatic cuss." Hardcastle said.

"All right, then," Clint said. "Midnight. Where?"

"In his number one laundry."

"Not in a casino? Or opium den?"

"He likes his laundry."

"Well," Clint said, "at least it'll be in a clean place. Why don't you play some blackjack while we wait?"

"I'd rather eat," Hardcastle said.

"Eating," Clint agreed, "is a good idea."

***

Ben Fong's No. 1 Laundry was down a darkened alley in Chinatown.

"He really does laundry?" Clint asked.

"As well as running casinos, opium dens and most of the tongs, yes."

"Tongs?"

"Gangs."

"Oh yes," Clint said, "I remember."

"So you've been here before," Hardcastle said.

"Once or twice, but it's been a while. I had some dealings with a Chinese gunman."

"That must've been unusual."

"It was. You don't often see a Chinese wearing a gun and holster."

"It's right down here," Hardcastle said, leading the way.

They came to a closed door, and he knocked on it. It was opened by a small, Chinese girl. Without raising her eyes, she stood aside and allowed them to enter. Then she closed the door and shuffled ahead of them. They followed.

She led them to a hot room that smelled of bleach. An older Chinaman wearing what looked like pajamas stood at an ironing board. When he saw them, he stepped away from it.

"Mr. Hardcastle," he said.

"Mr. Fong," Hardcastle said. "This is Clint Adams."

"That will be all, Mei Ling."

The girl, who still had never looked up, turned and hurried away.

"Mr. Adams," Ben Fong said, "it is a pleasure. Please forgive me for meeting here, but I find doing laundry very soothing after a difficult day."

"I'm sorry you had a difficult day," Clint said.

"I am Chinese," Fong said. "Every day is a difficult day. How may I help you?"

"It's come to my attention that there may be a war approaching on the Barbary Coast, involving The Red Lady and another house."

"What house might that be?"

"Well, I was hoping you could help me identify it. You see, someone has been trying to sabotage The Red Lady, and an attempt was made on the owner's life."

"I had heard of these things," Fong said.

"I was also hoping to determine, if such a war started, where you would stand."

"A war between two houses owned by *lo fan*?" Ben Fong said. "Why would I be involved, at all?"

"So you would just stand aside and watch."

Ben Fong raised his index finger and said, "And laugh."

"Then perhaps you can tell me what you've heard of this possibility."

"I have heard that The Red Lady is a very successful operation that has been having some difficulties."

"And have you heard anything about who has been behind these difficulties?"

"I have not."

"Would you offer a guess?" Clint asked. "Who do you think would benefit from The Red Lady's problems?"

Ben Fong spread his hands apart and said, "Everyone. I believe since the place opened, it has been taking business from all the other houses."

"Chinese houses?"

"No," Ben Fong said. "We do not cater to the same class of gambler. And the Chinese houses offer games you do not see in white casinos."

"So she's no competition to you at all?"

"None."

"And there's nothing helpful you can tell me?"

"I do not believe so," the Chinaman said. "Now, if you please, I wish to get back to my laundry."

"Thank you for your time."

Although Ben Fong did not call her, Mei Ling appeared to usher them out.

As they stepped out the door, Mei Ling looked up for the first time, revealing a lovely face.

"May I speak?"

"Of course," Clint said.

"If I were you," she said, "I would look for the man with two faces."

She closed the door before Clint could say a word.

Chapter Thirty

As they left the alley and looked for a cab to take them back to The Red Lady, Clint said, "The man with two faces?"

"Twins?" Hardcastle said.

"Of course," Clint said. "Another vote for the Slade brothers."

"Do we want to assume it's them?" Hardcastle asked.

"Let's wait until I see Muldoon tomorrow," Clint said. "I want to hear what he thinks."

"You're the boss."

"You think I'm playing it wrong?"

"I told you," Hardcastle said. "I don't like the law, but that's just me."

They waved down a passing cab and told the driver to take them to The Red Lady.

"That new place," the driver said, as they got in. "It's supposed to be pretty good."

"That's what we heard," Clint agreed.

***

The five hired men filed into a room while a single man waited there for them.

"Close that door," the man called.

One of the five men did that, then all five stood quietly waiting.

"Correct me if I'm wrong," the man at the head of the room said. "You're all for hire, and none of you have any qualms about what the job is."

"Qualms?" one man said, screwing up his face.

"Scruples," the headman said. "I mean none of you care what the job is as long as you are well paid."

All the men nodded their heads.

"What's the job?" another man asked.

"It involves some rough stuff," the headman said.

"How rough?" a voice called out.

"Doing damage to property and to people."

"That ain't rough stuff," another man said, "that's fun stuff."

They all laughed, and another voice said, "I don't care what I hafta do, as long as I'm gettin' paid."

"Then listen up," the headman said, "this is what I want you to do."

***

Clint and Hardcastle got back to The Red Lady late. They found Folsom just outside the casino entrance and noticed there was still activity inside.

"How's it goin'?" Folsom asked.

"All fingers are pointing to the Slade brothers," Clint said.

"They own The Barbary Queen, don't they?" Folsom asked.

"That's right."

"I wouldn't think their place would give this one any competition."

"It's the other way around," Clint said. "They could be losing business to this place."

"This place seems too high-class for sailors and long-shoremen."

"Still, most folks we talked to seem to think they can afford to hire the help needed, and their egos are big enough to think they're in competition with the Lady," Hardcastle said.

"Any trouble here tonight?" Clint asked.

"None," Folsom said. "Everythin's been quiet."

"Good, good," Clint said. "I'm going to walk around some before turning in."

"You don't need me for that, do ya?" Hardcastle asked.

"No," Clint said, "I feel pretty safe here."

"Then I'm turnin' in," Hardcastle said to both of them, "good-night."

As Hardcastle walked away, Folsom said, "I'll walk with ya. I've been doin' this the past coupla nights."

"Fine with me."

They talked as they walked the property.

"So whataya gonna do tomorrow?" Folsom asked.

"I'm going to check in with the police detective, Muldoon, and see what he's got. If he agrees it's the Slade brothers, I think we'll go and see them together."

"But you can't prove it's them," Folsom said.

"Maybe not," Clint said. "I just have to convince them that I'd move against them, proof or no proof. And Muldoon will say that the police are watching them. Hopefully, that'll be enough to call them off."

They stopped at the saloon, exchanged a nod with the man on duty. From there they checked the back doors, where two other men were on watch. The theater doors were locked, but they had a key to get in and looked around, then locked up again.

After that they went back to the casino.

"We're gonna close it down in about an hour," Folsom said. "Then we walk the folks out."

"That's fine with me," Clint said. "I'm going to turn in for the night. See you tomorrow."

" 'night, Clint."

Clint left Folsom standing at the casino entrance and went to his room.

Chapter Thirty-One

Clint had a good night's sleep, mostly because Delilah wasn't there when he reached his room. He slept lightly, in case she came to the door, but slept well. In fact, he was surprised when he woke the next morning, that she hadn't come to his room all night. As he dressed, he realized that Honey Roy wasn't sitting outside Genevieve's room when he passed it. So maybe Genevieve and Delilah were together, doing whatever they were doing. Maybe he'd find out at breakfast.

He went down to the dining room and found it empty. As he sat, Hardcastle appeared at the door and joined him.

"Just us this mornin'?" the man asked.

"I don't know," Clint said. "We'll see if anyone else shows up. If they don't, I'm going to start to worry."

But before the waiter could even bring their order, Genevieve and Honey Roy walked in and joined them.

"Where's Delilah this morning?" Clint asked.

"I'm afraid we stayed up late in the office, going over the books," Genevieve said. "By the time we quit, the casino was closed, everybody was gone or had gone off to bed. She was exhausted, and said she'd probably sleep late."

"Is there a problem with the books?" Clint asked.

"Not at all," Genevieve said. "Even with the extra expense of a security force, we're doing quite well."

"That's good to hear."

"What have you found out?"

"Most of the people we've talked to seem to think the Slade brothers are behind your difficulties."

"Slade," Genevieve said. "Those are the twins who own the Barbary Queen, right?"

"That's right."

"They really think we're taking some of their customers?"

"Apparently, their egos are big enough for them to think they're in competition with you."

"You know," she said, "more and more I'm starting to think we should have opened in Portsmouth Square, where there's room for everyone."

"It's true that the owners of the casinos there get along quite well," Clint said. "No funny business, there."

"So what will you do?" Genevieve asked, "if you have no proof?"

"I'll warn them off," Clint said. "Let them know we suspect them, and we'll be watching them."

"What about the police? That handsome Lieutenant Muldoon?" She threw a glance at Honey Roy seated at the door.

"I'll check in with him today. If he's come to the same conclusion, I'm sure we can go and see the Slade brothers together."

They were halfway through breakfast when Delilah arrived. She said good morning to Honey Roy, and then joined them at the table.

Bring me my usual," she told the waiter.

"Yes, Ma'am."

"Good morning, all," she greeted as she seated herself. "Sorry I'm late."

"Genevieve explained you were up late," Clint said.

"No later than she and Honey Roy, and they were here early," Delilah said. "I think I'm just gettin' old."

Clint doubted that Delilah was even thirty, yet.

"You're entitled to some extra sleep," Clint said.

"What did I miss?" she asked.

Clint went through the previous day's activities again.

"I never liked those Slade brothers," she said.

"You know them?" Clint asked.

"I worked for them for a short time," she said. "I especially disliked Dolph. Wait, is he the one with the scar? It's the one with the scar I dislike the most."

"So they know you work here?" Clint asked.

"I don't know," she said. "You don't think they're tryin' to sabotage us because I work here?"

"Who knows what their reasons might be?" Clint asked. "We haven't even confirmed that it was them, but it seems likely."

"What else have you got that points to them?" Delilah asked.

"That Chinee gal," Hardcastle said.

"A Chinese girl?" Delilah asked. "What did she have to say?"

"She said watch for the man with two faces," Hardcastle said.

"What the hell is that supposed that mean?" Genevieve asked.

"Seems like she's talkin' about twins," Hardcastle said.

Delilah looked at Clint.

"Why'd you talk to a Chinese girl about this?"

"We were talking to Ben Fong, who runs Chinatown," Clint corrected. "He said he didn't know anything, but there was a girl there who snuck us the information."

"About a man with two faces?"

"Yes."

"Why didn't she just say what she meant?" Genevieve asked, with a frown.

"I think she did," Clint said.

Chapter Thirty-Two

As Clint and Hardcastle headed for the front door, Delilah came running up from behind and grabbed Clint's right arm. He pulled it away.

"I didn't mean nothin', Clint," she said, quickly.

"I just can't have my gun arm being held," Clint said. "Got to be ready for trouble."

"Right, right," she said. "Sorry." She looked at Hardcastle.

"I'll be right there," Clint said.

"Right."

Hardcastle went out the door.

"I'm sorry I didn't come by last night," she said.

"I understand," Clint said. "You were tired. So was I. I'll see you later."

"I hope you get this settled today," she said.

"I hope so, too."

He went out the front door, nodded to Leo as he passed. Hardcastle was waiting by the street.

"Where to first?" Hardcastle asked.

"The police station."

"I'll be in the saloon across the way."

"Suits me."

They flagged a cab and took it to the police station.

***

When Muldoon came out to meet Clint, he was wearing his suit—jacket and all.

"No office today?" Clint asked.

"Let's talk in the saloon across the street," Muldoon said.

"A little early for me," Clint said. "I'll have coffee."

"I'm Irish," Muldoon said. "Never too early for me."

They left the building together and walked across the street.

When Hardcastle saw them enter together he ignored them, turned his back to the room and leaned on the bar.

Clint got coffee, Muldoon whiskey, and they took a table in the mostly empty saloon.

"What've ya got?" Muldoon asked.

"I talked to most of the houses in Portsmouth Square, and to Ben Fong in Chinatown."

"Fong," Muldoon said. "How'd you get onto him?"

"Somebody sent me his way."

"What'd he have to say?"

"Nothing," Clint said. "yet I did get the same name from a couple of the casino owners."

"What name?"

"What'd you get?"

"I got one name, two people," Muldoon said. "The Slade brothers."

"That's who I got."

"Any proof?" Muldoon asked.

"Just guesses."

"Same here," Muldoon said. "If it is them, they didn't get their own hands dirty."

"Do they have a regular crew they use?"

"Three men," Muldoon said, "but they left town."

"After the fires?"

Muldoon nodded.

"Paid off and sent on their way, I imagine," Clint said. "So they couldn't talk."

"That's what I figured."

"I'm going to talk to them," Clint said.

"You're not gonna kill 'em?"

Clint shook his head.

"Just warn them off," Clint said. "Be happy to have company."

"What about that fella at the bar?" Muldoon said.

"You've got a good eye."

"I have a suggestion, Adams."

"Let's hear it."

"We go see the Slades separately. They know I'm limited in what I can do by the law. They will also know you have no such limits, if you get my meaning."

"You want them to think I might kill them."

"Exactly."

"That suits me," Clint said. "Who goes in first?"

"I will," Muldoon said. "You and your friend can go soon after."

"Agreed."

Muldoon downed his whiskey and stood.

"I'll head over there right now."

"Taking somebody to watch your back?" Clint asked.

"I'll have two men with me."

"Sounds good," Clint said.

"Let's compare notes at the end of the day. I'll meet you here at six,"

"That's a deal."

Muldoon left the saloon, and Clint joined Hardcastle at the bar.

"What's goin' on?" Hardcastle asked.

"Muldoon's going to hit the Slades first, and then we follow up."

"Good," Hardcastle said, waving at the bartender, "time for another drink."

Chapter Thirty-Three

Clint and Hardcastle gave Detective Muldoon two hours to collect his men and get over to The Barbary Queen. When they were across the street from the saloon, they saw Muldoon and his two men come out. If the detective saw them, he ignored them. After the three policemen had climbed into their wagon and left, Clint and Hardcastle crossed the street and entered. They didn't bother stopping at the bar but headed straight for the office.

"Hey!" the bartender yelled. "Hey, you can't—"

Clint pointed his finger at the bartender, and the man fell silent.

"Just stay there and don't move."

The bartender put his hands up and nodded. Some of the gamblers looked over at them, but then turned their attentions back to their games.

When Clint and Hardcastle reached the office door, they opened it without warning and entered. Only one of the Slade brothers was there, the one with the scarred face. Clint hadn't expected that.

"What the hell do you want?" the man asked.

"Are you Danny or Dolph?" Clint asked.

"Does it matter?"

"Not really."

"Say what you came to say."

"I saw a policeman coming out of here when I arrived," Clint said. "What was on his mind?"

"Same thing that's on yours, I imagine," Slade said. "He thinks my brother and me got it in for The Red Lady. That what you think?"

"It is."

"Well, he can't do nothin' about it, since he's the law and he needs proof."

"Well, we're not the law and we don't need proof."

Slade was standing behind his desk and when he took a step back, he bumped into the wall.

"Are you sayin' you'd kill us on a hunch? A rumor?"

"I just might," Clint said, "if any other harm should befall The Red Lady—the place or the woman. Understood?"

"Oh, I understand you," Slade said. "You'd murder us, and expect to get away with it, is that right?"

"Now you understand," Clint said.

"Well, you better do it real quiet like, because the police are gonna be watcin' us,"

"Why do I get the feeling they'd just look the other way?" Clint asked.

Slade looked alarmed.

"I doubt that."

"I guess we'll see," Clint said. "Just remember, the police aren't the only ones watching you."

Clint and Hardcastle turned and left the office. As they passed the bartender, he put his hands in the air, again.

After they went out the batwing doors they stopped momentarily.

"Think he got the message?" Hardcastle asked.

"I'm sure he did," Clint said. "I just wish his brother had been there. I think he's the backbone of the pair."

"What makes you say that?"

"Just a feeling I get."

"So, do we wanna come back and see him?"

"Maybe we do."

"And which one is he?"

Clint raised his eyebrows.

"I still don't know which is which," he admitted, rubbing his chin. "Maybe that's something we ought to find out."

"There's an easy way to do that," Hardcastle said. "Let's go back inside."

They turned and went back in.

"Wait here," Hardcastle said, and went to the bar.

While he waited Clint looked over the operation. Anywhere else this would probably be considered a first-rate joint. But with Portsmouth Square so nearby, the Barbary Queen suffered by comparison.

After a conversation with the bartender, Hardcastle returned, and they stepped outside, again.

"We just talked to Dolph," he said. "Danny is the clean-faced one."

"And which one carries the most weight?"

"The bartender says that's Danny."

"Well then, Dolph's going to have to tell Danny we were here and what was said."

"And then Danny can decide what to do," Hardcastle said.

"Call off his dogs," Clint said, "or escalate the aggression."

"Escalate?"

"Beef it up," Clint said.

"You think he'd do that?" Hardcastle asked. "After the law and us were here?"

"If he's got more sand than his brother," Clint said, "yeah, I do."

"So whatta we do?"

"Beef up security," Clint said, "just in case we lit a fuse here today."

Chapter Thirty-Four

As planned, Clint met with Detective Muldoon at the saloon across the street from the police station. Since it was now obvious that many of the customers were policemen, Hardcastle remained outside.

Clint and Muldoon exchanged stories of their meeting with Dolph Slade.

"He's the more dimwitted of the two," Muldoon said.

"That's what I figured," Clint said. "I wish Danny had been there. Now we just have to guess what he'll do when Dolph tells him about our visits."

"If I was you," Muldoon said, "I'd beef up my security until we can determine what his actions will be."

"I'll take that advice," Clint said. "I assume we're both still convinced it was them."

"I can't think of anyone else," Muldoon said, "unless it's somebody from the outside. Has anybody made an offer to buy her out?"

"I'd have to ask her that," Clint said. "I haven't heard of any such offer."

"Well, if you do," Muldoon said, "let me know."

"I'll do that."

Muldoon stood up and left. Clint finished his beer and followed, found Hardcastle lounging against the wall outside.

"What's his take on it?" he asked.

"Same as ours," Clint said. "He also suggests we increase security until we see what Danny Slade decides what to do."

"I'll ask Duke for a few more men," Clint said.

"I can take care of that."

"Men who'll take orders from Folsom?" Clint asked.

"Folsom, the Red Lady, you," Hardcastle said. "They'll do what they're told. I'll have 'em in place by tomorrow."

"We might as well get back, then," Clint said. "If Danny Slade is not the type to get scared off, he'll be trying something soon."

***

Once Clint was safe inside The Red Lady, Hardcastle left to rustle up the extra men. Clint had a beer in the saloon while he decided where to place the new men. Before long, Delilah joined him at the bar.

"You look like you got something on your mind," she said.

He looked sideways at her, admiring her profile. As usual, she was wearing a purple gown.

"When are you going to come clean?" he asked.

"When am I gonna what?"

"Tell the truth."

"About what?"

"About who owns this place," Clint said. "Genevieve looks the part, but she's not smart enough to run this operation. You're the Red Lady, aren't you?"

"What gave me away?" she asked, not bothering to deny it.

"You just have the air of someone who's in charge," he said. "Genevieve is just a pretty woman in a red dress, who can sing. Where'd you find her?"

"I brought her here with me, figuring she looked the part. I wanted to be able to make moves without anyone knowing this place was mine."

"Do you intend to come out from behind your purple dress, at some point?"

"I guess that'll depend on what happens," she replied. "And on how long Gen's nerve holds out."

"Is she the nervous type?"

"She's getting there," Delilah said. "Having Honey Roy by her side is helping, though."

"I think he's been more than just at her side."

"Oh, I know she's fucking him," Delilah said. "I don't mind, as long as he keeps her safe, and calm."

"We're going to bring in some more men tomorrow," Clint said.

"Why more?"

"If the Slade brothers are behind all this, we might've lit a fuse under them."

"So you figure they'll try somethin' soon?" she asked.

"I'm hoping they will, so we can put this whole matter to rest, and you can conduct business with no fear."

"And will you be leaving San Francisco then?"

"Not yet," Clint said. "I haven't had time to relax, yet."

"Gambling and drinking?"

"And more."

"Am I included in that more?"

"If you'd like to be."

"I hope this all ends real soon," she said. "I could use some of that relaxation myself."

"You know," Clint said, "I'd like to see you in a red dress."

"That can be arranged," she told him.

He turned to face her and added, "And then out of it."

"Well," she said, "that can be arranged as well. But let's start with a drink."

She waved to the bartender, and he brought her a glass of champagne.

Chapter Thirty-Five

Clint was sitting in the saloon with Delilah when Hardcastle returned.

"I'll leave you two to talk," she said, walking away.

Hardcastle took her seat.

"It's all set," he said. "There'll be four more men here tomorrow. All good hands with a gun."

"Fine."

Clint waved to the bartender for two beers. The man carried them over and set them down.

"Anythin' else for today?" Hardcastle asked.

"I don't think so," Clint said. "If the Slade brothers don't make a move soon, we're going to have to look elsewhere for our culprits. So I'm hoping it's them."

"If it's not," Hardcastle said, "we're going to be here a damn long time."

"I'm not going to pin it on them just to get it finished," Clint said.

"I wouldn't expect you to. Can we take the time to get a meal?"

"You go ahead," Clint said. "I'm going to sit here a while."

Hardcastle nodded, drained his beer, and left the saloon for the dining room.

Clint sat back in his chair and considered his options. He didn't know who else there was to question. If the brains behind the attempts on The Red Lady was an outsider, then the only way to identify him was to find one of the men that was hired for the job. It was entirely possible that a man they were paying for security could have been one of the saboteurs, although he doubted that Duke Farrell would have recommended such a man.

But maybe one of their hired men would know the type of person who would hire out to do damage or kill.

Clint decided to broach the subject with Folsom and the other men, finished his beer and went to do so.

***

Danny Slade listened to his brother's account of his meetings with Detective Muldoon and Clint Adams.

"Fuck!" was his immediate reaction.

"Danny—"

"Fuck, Dolph!" Danny snapped. "All you had to do was keep your mouth shut."

"I didn't tell them anything!" Dolph insisted.

Danny sat back in his chair and glared up at his brother. He was well acquainted with the scar, because he had put it there when they were ten.

"We still gonna go ahead?" Dolph asked.

"Damn right, we are," Danny said. "I'm not lettin' no modern policeman and Old West legend affect our business. We're takin' that Red Lady down, board-by-board."

"When?"

"That's what I gotta figure, brother," Danny said, "that's what I gotta figure."

***

"There are any number of men who'd take a job like that," Folsom told him.

"Can you name any?" Clint asked.

"Let's give it some thought," Folsom said, "but I'd hate to label somebody who don't deserve it."

"See what you can get me by tomorrow," Clint said. "Meanwhile, we're bringing in some more men."

"Expectin' trouble?" Folsom asked.

"Always," Clint said.

He talked with the other men, and while they all had suggestions, the same name was never mentioned twice.

Talking with all the security men caused Clint to have a very late dinner in an empty dining room.

"Sorry to keep you and the cook so late," he told the waiter.

"That's okay, Mr. Adams. We'll close up as soon as you're done, but don't rush."

A bowl of beef stew was the easiest and fastest thing to order, along with a basket of biscuits and a mug of beer to wash it down.

He was almost finished when Genevieve and Honey Roy walked in. The ex-fighter remained by the door as the woman in red approached him and sat.

"Delilah told me she told you our arrangement."

"She did."

"And you understand it?"

"I do."

"Well, it's nice not to have to pretend anymore, with you."

"I just wonder why you'd agree to such an arrangement," Clint said.

"Nobody ever thought of me as a lady before," she confided. "So bein' The Red Lady was appealin'. Also, she's payin' me good money for the play actin'."

"And the singing."

"That I insisted on," Genevieve said.

"There's no play actin' about that," he said. "You sing very well."

"Thank you very kindly, sir," she said. "And may I say, if I wasn't fuckin' Honey Roy, I'd've been throwin' one your way, by now."

"I appreciate that," he replied, "but I think I've got all I can handle with Delilah."

"That's good, then," she said. "I just wanted to talk to somebody as the real me, with no play actin' involved. Bein' a lady is hard work."

"The real you is fine with me, Genevieve."

"Just call me Gen," she said, stood up and left, with Honey Roy close behind.

Clint finished his dinner and went to his room. When he entered, Delilah sat up in his bed, the sheet down to her waist so he could see her full, pink-tipped breasts.

"You ready?"

"Genevieve just offered to toss me one and I said no," Clint said, removing his gunbelt and shirt. "What do you think?"

Chapter Thirty-Six

The next morning after breakfast four more men showed up at the door and Leo brought them in to see Clint. From appearances they looked competent, so Clint put them together with Folsom, to place them strategically throughout the operation.

Hardcastle stood up and said, "I'll help Folsom with that."

"Fine," Clint said, "I'll be here having more coffee while I figure what our next move is."

"Seems to me our next move is just sittin' and waitin'," Hardcastle said, "but that's just my opinion. It's gonna be your decision."

Hardcastle left, passing some customers just coming in.

Since the dining room was about to get busy for breakfast, Clint finished his coffee and left. He didn't see what he could accomplish by leaving the building. It seemed best to just sit and wait for another attempt. He might have thought different, but the recent fires seemed to indicate the Slade brothers—if, indeed, it was them—were growing impatient.

Delilah came walking into the lobby while Clint was pacing.

"What's on your mind?" she asked. "You look worried."

"Concerned, is more like it," Clint said. "I'm just wondering when the next attempt is going to come."

"Do you think we should put Genevieve outside to lure them in?" Delilah asked.

"I wouldn't want to use her as bait that way," Clint said. "It might get her killed, which wouldn't accomplish a thing."

"Except maybe bring somebody out into the open."

"She told me you were paying her well, but I don't think it's well enough to get killed. We'll do it another way."

"How?"

"That's what I'm thinking about."

"Maybe some time upstairs would help you with your thinking?" she suggested.

"Some time with you upstairs would take my mind off of everything *but* you."

"I could throw a red dress into the offer."

"That's tempting," he said, "but I'd hate for another attempt to be made while you and I were occupied."

"I get your meaning," she said. "Rest assured there's a red dress in our future."

"I'm looking forward to that."

"I've got to go and see Gen about some business," Delilah said.

"I'll see you later," Clint said.

She touched his left arm and then moved along.

***

Dolph Slade came into the office and looked at his brother, seated behind their desk.

"The boys are here," he said.

"How many?"

"Six."

"We need more."

"How many more?" Dolph asked.

"I think they're gettin' themselves ready for another attempt," Danny said. "I want a dozen, Dolph."

"Six more?"

"That's right," Danny said. "I want to go all out, this time."

"That's gonna take a little longer."

"You go out there and tell each of those boys to bring one man back with them," Danny said. "That'll get the number doubled."

"And what're you gonna do?"

"I'm gonna sit right here," Danny told him, "and come up with a foolproof plan to burn that Red Lady place to the ground."

Chapter Thirty-Seven

Clint knew the casino would be getting busy, as was the dining room. But there were no shows in the theater until later in the day, so he went there and sat in a seat in the back.

When he heard the theater door open, he almost drew his gun before he saw Detective Muldoon walk in.

"This was the last place I looked," Muldoon said. He sat in a seat, leaving one empty between them.

"I noticed you brought in some extra men."

"Yes, I did," Clint said. "I want us to be ready for anything."

"That's good thinkin," Muldoon said. "I had a man watching the Slades place. He said half a dozen men went inside, and then came out, very quickly."

"Quick in and out?" Clint asked. "Could it be those men were sent in search of more men?"

"My thought exactly," Muldoon said. "My guess would be a dozen or so."

"Well, I've got enough men to fight them off," Clint said.

"You'll have to see them coming," Muldoon said. "You'd be well advised to put some eyes on the roof."

"Good suggestion," Clint said, and thought he and Folsom had already done so.

"So are you staying inside from this point on?" Muldoon asked.

"I'm still thinking about it."

"All you could do other than waiting here is going after them like folks think the Gunsmith would do."

"You mean killing them?"

"That's what I mean."

"And you'd look the other way?"

Muldoon stood up.

"I can't arrest you for something I don't see," he said, and left.

"Now Clint had something else to think about.

***

"Would you do that?" Hardcastle asked him, sometime later.

"Muldoon was right," Clint said, "that's what people would expect the Gunsmith to do."

"But?"

"I pride myself on not killing anyone who's not trying to kill me."

"If they come, and you're here, they'll be tryin' to kill you."

"That's true enough."

"And if you walk into their place alone, they'll probably also try."

"That's fair to say."

"But if you stay here, you're defending The Red Lady," Hardcastle went on. "If you walk into their place, your baitin' them."

"You've got it all straight in your head," Clint observed.

"I say wait," Hardcastle said. "They'll be comin'. And if it's not them, then whoever it is will come. And when they do, you'll know you're in the right. If you just go over there and kill 'em, you'll never know." Hardcastle downed the glass of whiskey on the table in front of him. "So yeah, I've got it straight in my head."

Clint sipped from his beer as they sat at a back table.

"We put two men on the roof," Clint said. "We should see them coming."

"That's good," Hardcastle said. "I assume whoever comes we'll use deadly force, so nobody ever tries it again."

"Right."

Hardcastle nodded, poured himself another drink. He held the glass up.

"Here's to deadly force."

Clint lifted his mug and they clinked glasses.

***

Dolph and Danny Slade looked at the twelve men seated before them.

"You," Danny said, pointing at one man. He was an Indian. It didn't matter to Danny what tribe he was from.

"Can you move around without bein' seen?" Danny asked.

"I am like a ghost," the man said.

"Even in San Francisco?"

"There are many in San Francisco who people would not want to see," the Indian said. "Chinee, Irish, my people, we all blend in."

"What's your name?"

"Johnny Blue."

"Well, Johnny," Danny said, "I want you to go over to The Red Lady and assess their security."

"I would not be able to go inside, and remain unseen," Blue said.

"That's okay," Danny said. "I want to know what they've got outside."

"I can do that."

"Then go do it!"

Johnny Blue stood up and left the room.

"Now, the rest of you," Danny said, "this is what Dolph and me want . . ."

Chapter Thirty-Eight

Clint asked Delilah and Genevieve to take dinner with him that night. Honey Roy sat at a table by the door, aiming to eat his alone. He asked Hardcastle to also attend, but the man refused. He considered Clint was working with the two women, and he was just along to watch Clint's back. So he sat with Honey Roy.

Clint explained the situation to both women, while they listened attentively.

"So you're expecting some kind of an attack," Delilah said, when he was done.

"An actual attack?" Genevieve asked. "So they won't be sneakin' around, anymore?"

"I hope not."

"You mean," Genevieve asked, "you want them to attack us?"

"I mean, we're ready for it," Clint said, "with the extra men."

"So what are we supposed to do?" Delilah asked.

"When it happens," Clint said, "I want both of you to stay close to Honey Roy until it's over."

"And will it be over, if they come?" Genevieve asked.

"We'll make it be over," Clint assured her.

***

Dolph entered the office, said to his brother Danny, "Johnny Blue's back."

"Get 'im in here."

Danny sat back in his chair and waited for the Indian to enter the office.

"What've you got, Johnny?"

"They have a man on the door, two on the roof, and two in the back."

"Any idea what's inside?" Danny asked.

"No. That is all I saw."

"Okay," Danny said, "go and have a drink."

The Indian nodded and left.

"Five in the outside," Dolph said, "How many do you think on the inside?"

"At least that," Danny said.

"So whatta we do?"

"We take the outside ones first," Danny said, "then we'll outnumber the insides."

"Are you sure?"

"How the fuck can I be sure, Dolph?" Danny snapped. "That's what I figure."

"Well," Dolph said, "your figurin' has always been right up to now."

"Yes," Danny said, "it has."

"So when do we move?"

"We'll let 'em wait a while," Danny said. "Make 'em nervous."

"I got a question."

"What is it?" Danny asked.

"That Muldoon came here, and then Adams and Hardcastle," Dolph said. "If they know it's us, why don't they just come here and kill us?"

"That's a good question," Danny said. "My guess is they don't wanna cross the law."

"You think the Gunsmith cares about the law?" Dolph asked.

"From everything I've heard about him," Danny replied, "I never heard he was a lawbreaker. But just in case, put a few of the men out front."

"Right."

"Now get those men situated out in front," Danny said. "I wanna know if they're comin'."

"You think the Gunsmith's gonna come for us?" Dolph asked.

"I dunno," Danny said, "but there's no harm in bein' ready. Meanwhile, we'll make our own plan."

Dolph knew he didn't have to give the event any thought. Danny would plan the whole thing.

***

Clint went up to the roof to take a look at the sights.

The two men on the roof were Chester and Mike. Folsom knew them, so it wasn't necessary for Clint to know their last names.

They stood a roof length apart from each other, watching the street below. Clint joined each man for a short time, then went back downstairs and met up with Hardcastle.

"I checked with the two men watchin' the back," Hardcastle said. "Nothin' yet."

"They're going to make us wait," Clint said. "They're thinking they'll make us nervous."

"Then they don't know who they're dealin' with," Hardcastle said.

"The one big advantage we have is their egos," Clint said. "They feel as if they're in control."

"The one who should feel in control and have an ego is you," Hardcastle said, "and you don't."

"I've never been able to afford an ego," Clint said. "That's a sure way to get killed."

Chapter Thirty-Nine

After two days, the ones who started to get nervous were Delilah and Genevieve.

"When is this going to happen?" Delilah asked at breakfast.

"They're making us wait," Clint said. "They want you asking questions like that."

"But they are gonna come soon, aren't they?" Genevieve asked.

"I'm sure they are," Clint said, "if they feel you're taking some of their trade."

"Are we?" Delilah asked. "Or do they just think it? Or fear it?"

"Gus and I discussed their egos," Clint said. "They believe they're on a level with you, which makes them think they're losing trade to you, whether they are or not."

"So this is all because of the ego of two men," Delilah said.

"More likely, the ego of one man," Clint said. "They may be twins in appearance, but I think the brains all went to one of them."

"Brains and ego?" Genevieve asked.

"A deadly combination," Clint said.

"So what do we do in the meantime?" Delilah asked.

"Go back to work," Clint said. "And stay there until something happens."

"How will we know?" Genevieve asked.

"Don't worry," Clint said. "You'll know."

***

Hardcastle and Honey Roy had their own conversation about their situation.

"I'd like to do more to help," Honey Roy said.

"You're doin' what you can," Hardcastle said.

"I fuck her when she asks me to," Honey Roy said, "Or rather, when she tells me to. That's all I've done, so far."

"Well, your presence will be important when the attack comes."

"And you believe it will soon?"

"Very soon," Hardcastle said. "I believe they've kept us waitin' long enough."

"Then I'll be ready."

"Do you have a gun?" Hardcastle asked.

"I have one that Clint gave me," Honey Roy said, "but I'm much better with my hands. If anyone tries to harm Miss Genevieve, I'll break them in half."

"I'm sure you can do it," Hardcastle said. "Me, I'm just a hand with a gun."

"As good as Clint?" Honey Roy asked.

"I doubt that, but good enough."

"Watchin' him in action is gonna be somethin' to see," Honey Roy said.

"Ain't it, though," Hardcastle said.

***

Genevieve stopped at Honey Roy's table to take him with her. She gave Hardcastle a nod on the way out. Then Delilah walked by and smiled at him. That left Clint alone at his table, so Hardcastle got up and joined him, taking his cup of coffee with him.

"Are they ready?" he asked.

"Pretty much," Clint said. "What about Honey Roy?"

"He's lookin' to do somethin' else, other than fucking Genevieve."

"Well, it's coming," Clint said.

"I think I'm gonna spend some time on the roof," Hardcastle said. "I mean, if we ain't leavin' here, today."

"I think we'll give it one more day," Clint said, "and then give it a push."

"By goin' back to The Barbary Queen to see the Slades?"

"To see Danny," Clint said. "He's got to be the man in charge."

"And what if we're totally wrong, and it's not them?" Hardcastle asked.

"Then I read this whole thing wrong, and The Red Lady needs to hire somebody new to get out of this mess."

"I hope that ain't the case," Hardcastle said. He finished his coffee, put his cup down and stood up. "I'll be seein' you later."

Clint watched Hardcastle leave the dining room, then stood and followed.

***

Clint went to the front door, stepped out and beckoned to Leo.

"Yes, Sir?"

"Leo," Clint asked, "are you satisfied to be on this door yourself?"

"I have been, up to now," Leo said.

"There may be more trouble than you've dealt with so far," Clint said. "I can put another man, with a gun, here with you for the foreseeable future. Would you want that?"

Leo thought a moment, then said, "I believe I would, Sir."

"Done!" Clint said. "A man will be here within the hour."

Chapter Forty

On the table in front of Danny Slade was a large drawing, depicting The Red Lady and its environs.

"I want the two on the roof first," he said, pointing. "Here, and here. Understood?"

His twelve hired men all nodded their understanding.

"Then I want their bodies left up there so nobody sees them."

More nods.

"What about the two watching the back?" one man asked.

"Find a way to the roof without going to the back," Danny said. "From either side is more likely."

"Then what?" another man asked.

"Johnny Blue says there's one man on the front door," Slade said. "I expect they'll put one more, there. They'll have to be dealt with before we can get inside."

All the man nodded and stared at the drawing.

"Timing'll be important," Danny went on. "You men on the roof must not go in until the men on the front door are dealt with. Then you'll all go in at the same time. Got it?"

All the men nodded.

"You'll all follow Johnny Blue."

"Why's the Indian in charge?" another man asked.

"Because he's a better man than any of you," Danny said. "When this is all over, any man he tells me didn't heed his words, I'll kill, myself."

Danny rolled the drawing up and set it aside, then leaned on the table and looked at each of the twelve men.

"I want this done tomorrow night," he said. "I want The Red Lady burned to the ground. And I want it done during business hours."

"And the people inside?"

"Let them worry about gettin' out." He straightened. "A free drink for each of you. Then you stay sober til this is over. I find one of you passed out drunk, you won't wake up."

All twelve men stood and filed out. Dolph had been standing quietly in a corner. Now he stepped forward.

"Is this gonna work?" he asked his brother.

"It better," Danny said. "It fuckin' better."

***

Johnny Blue watched as the other eleven men had their free drink.

"One for you, Johnny?" the bartender asked.

"No."

174

"He's a damned Indian," one of the men said. "He don't drink."

Johnny Blue stared at the man, expressionless, causing him to turn his gaze to the bar.

***

As the day got older, Clint started to think they were clear one more day.

"What are you thinking?" Delilah asked. She was lying next to him in his bed.

"I don't think anythin' is going to happen tonight," he said, "but you should go back to your room, anyway."

"And you?"

"I'm going to walk around some," Clint said, "make sure everything is secure."

"You could come to my room after."

"I don't want to take a chance on being distracted."

"All right."

She stood up and got dressed.

"I'll see you in the morning?" she asked.

"Definitely."

She left the room and he listened to her footsteps as she went down the hall to her own room. Undoubtedly, Honey Roy was also watching from his chair.

Clint got up, dressed and strapped on his gun. He grabbed his hat on the way to the door and stepped into the hall. He started for the stairs, stopped when he came to Honey Roy.

"When's the last time you slept in a bed?" Clint asked.

"Night before you got me this job."

"Why don't you go inside?"

"Miss Genevieve don't want me in there. She can't sleep with somebody else in the bed. She just wants to sleep in her room, and fuck in her office."

"That's a woman who knows what she wants."

"Yes, sir."

Honey Roy still thought Genevieve was The Red Lady. Clint allowed it to remain that way. Delilah would pick her own time and date to come out from behind her purple dresses.

"I'm taking a turn around the property before I turn in," Clint said.

"See you on the way back," Honey Roy said.

Clint continued to the stairs. He knew the ex-fighter would be awake when he made his way back.

Chapter Forty-One

Clint ate breakfast alone the next morning. Neither Delilah nor Genevieve put in an appearance, and Hardcastle was also among the missing. After he finished, he went to Hardcastle's room and knocked on the door. When there was no answer, he recalled Hardcastle saying he was going to the roof.

On the roof he found the two men assigned there, but no Hardcastle. When questioned, both men said they hadn't seen him.

Clint left the roof and went through the entire complex, but there was no sign of Hardcastle. He went back to the man's room, afraid of what he would find inside, but when he forced the door, he found that the man had probably not spent the night there.

"Problem?" Honey Roy asked from his position in front of Genevieve's door.

"Have you seen Hardcastle?" Clint asked.

"Not this mornin'," Honey Roy said. "I thought he was sleepin' in."

"So you saw him come to his room last night?"

"Now that you mention it," Honey Roy said, "no."

"Is Gen in her room?" Clint asked.

"Definitely."

"Have you seen Delilah this morning?"

"No, not this morning," Honey Roy said.

"Last night?"

"When she came out of your room."

Clint nodded, turned and went back to Delilah's door. He knocked, then pounded. He was about to force the door when suddenly it opened and Delilah stared at him, bleary-eyed.

"Christ," she said, "what time is it?"

"Ten aye-em," Clint said. "You missed breakfast. In fact, everyone missed breakfast but me."

"What's going on?"

"I don't know," Clint said. "But I want to find out. Get dressed."

"Give me a minute," she said, and closed the door.

He waited in the hall for ten minutes, and then she came out, wearing her purple dress.

"What's first?"

"I want to see if Gen's in her room," Clint said. "Do you have a key?"

"No."

"Then I'll force the door."

"If she doesn't answer your knock," Delilah said.

"Right."

They walked to her door and stopped. Honey Roy stood up. Clint knocked on the door once, and then again. He was about to pound when she opened it, looking as bleary-eyed as Delilah had looked.

"What the hell?"

"You weren't at breakfast," Clint said. "I was worried."

Genevieve looked at Delilah.

"Hey, he woke me up, too."

"Now that we're all awake, when's the last time either of you saw Hardcastle?"

"Last night," Delilah said.

"Me, too," Genevieve said, through a yawn.

"Is he missing?" Delilah asked.

"Do you think he might've gone after the Slades?" Honey Roy asked.

"He could have," Clint answered. "I'll check with Leo on the front door and see if he left."

As Clint went down the stairs to the lobby, he didn't like the obvious other likelihood, that someone inside the building had harmed Hardcastle.

***

Leo said Hardcastle had not gone past him. Next Clint checked with the two men covering the rear of the buildings, and neither of them had seen him, either.

He did a complete check of the place and found nothing. He then went to Genevieve's office and found her there with Delilah.

"Any luck?" Delilah asked.

"None," Clint said. "It's as if he just vanished."

"Or . . . Honey Roy said.

They all looked at him.

"Or what?" Clint asked.

"Did it occur to you that maybe he just ran?" Honey Roy asked.

"He still would have to have gone past Leo on the door," Clint said.

"Or out a window," Honey Roy said.

"All the windows in the buildings are sealed," Delilah said. "They don't open."

"So now what?" Delilah asked.

"We'll just have to see if he shows up," Clint said.

"What if," Honey Roy asked, "if he shows up on the other side?"

Clint stared at the man and then said, "I'll deal with that if it happens."

Chapter Forty-Two

Clint spent most of the day hoping Hardcastle would show up. By dinner time he decided to give up waiting. If the man appeared, so be it. As to which side he would appear on, that remained to be seen—if he showed up, at all. Honey Roy's suggestion might have been true, that the man decided to walk away from the whole mess.

It grew dark outside, and the casino filled. Activities on the outside commenced . . .

***

Johnny Blue had two men move along the alley to the left of The Red Lady, carrying a ladder between them that would reach the high roof. The citizens of the area did not give them a second look.

Johnny sent two more men to the rear of the building, armed with pistols, but also with knives for silent mayhem. And three men were charged with the front, whether there was one man on the door, or two. It was all timed to coincide with Johnny Blue's estimation of how long the men with the ladder would take to reach the roof and perform their tasks.

***

Clint had stopped searching for Hardcastle and had stopped hoping the man would show up and explain his absence. Up to this point the man had seemed satisfied to simply back Clint's play. If he had changed his mind, that was certainly his right. If, indeed, he did reappear, he would no doubt have an explanation. But Clint needed to move on and be ready for whatever move Dolph and Danny Slade put into effect.

It was early evening. The Red Lady had two theaters. In one Genevieve was singing, and in the other an acting troupe was putting on a Shakespeare play. Clint had a man on security in each theater, but for the most part the audiences seemed to actually be interested in what was happening on stage.

Likewise, there might be trouble from a bad loser or two, on this night everyone seemed to either be happy with how their luck was going, or able to withstand their bad luck, hoping it would change.

The dining room was filled with satisfied diners.

The saloon was catering to before and after dinner drinkers, as well as gamblers—mostly male—who were trying to either build up their nerve before gambling or drinking away their bad luck.

Clint ran into Folsom in the lobby between the dining room and casino.

"It's quiet," Clint said.

"Too quiet," Folsom said. "Did you find Hardcastle yet?"

"Not a sign," Clint reported.

"Very strange," Folsom said. "I know the man pretty well. This is odd behavior."

"I agree," Clint said, "but don't have the time to continue worrying. I have to deal with what's actually happening now."

"Then I'll do the same," Folsom said. "Are you satisfied with the man I sent to watch the door with Leo?"

"I was on my way there now," Clint said. "I'll let you know if I have a problem."

"Then I'll see you later."

They went their separate ways.

***

Clint poked his head out the front door to take a look at Leo and the second man. The ex-fighter spotted him and came over.

"Is all well between you two?" Clint asked.

"We're gettin' along okay."

"No trouble?"

"Everyone requesting entry wants to gamble, eat, or attend the theater. No trouble, so far."

"Stay alert."

"Yes, sir."

Clint withdrew his head and closed the door. Just inside stood one of Delilah's girls, who would fetch him if there was trouble. She smiled at him, and he touched the brim of his hat.

***

The two men positioned the ladder, leaning it against the side of the building. They glanced both ways, but the alley had very little in the way of foot traffic, according to Johnny Blue.

One man held the bottom of the ladder while the other man began to ascend.

***

Two of the Slade men in the rear of The Red Lady kept a wary eye out but, also according to Johnny Blue, nobody ever took that route as a thoroughfare or short cut. And it was only on occasion of discarding garbage that anyone came from the rear of the Lady. The two security men stood at opposite ends, which would make them easy to take, one at a time.

***

It was now dark. In the front, from across the street, two Slade men watched the entrance and the two men assigned to it. One man kept a wary eye on his watch, attending to the timing assigned to them by Johnny Blue.

"Five minutes," he said.

The second man nodded. He saw someone stick their head out the door and hold a short conversation with one of the men, then withdraw.

"We'll be ready," he said.

***

The Slade brothers were in their office, Danny behind the desk, and Dolph across from him.

Danny looked at his pocket watch and said, "Any minute now."

"Are you sure this will work?" Dolph asked.

"It'll work," Danny said. "After tonight, The Red Lady will no longer be a problem for us."

Dolph wasn't sure, but he hoped his brother was right.

Chapter Forty-Three

The Slade man stood on almost the top rung of the ladder and peered over the edge. He saw no one. Apparently, the two men assigned to the roof patrolled it, which meant there were sections that were not patrolled for short periods of time. At the moment, this was one of them. The man quickly went from the ladder to the roof, then signaled for his partner to come up while he anchored the ladder. In moments, they were both on the roof. They turned, palmed their knives, and moved into the darkness. There was hardly any moonlight, and at the other end of the roof they could see the light from the oil lamps the security men were carrying. It looked like, at that moment, the men were standing together.

The two Slade men moved toward the light.

***

The Slade men in the rear of the Lady were ready. One of them peered at his watch using the light from a lit match and said, "It's time."

"Right," the other man said, "let's move."

They doused the match and moved into the darkness.

***

One of the two men across the street looked at his watch.

"One minute," he said.

"Where are the others?" the second man asked.

"Once we get the front door open, they'll come a-runnin'," the second man said. "That'll mean we gained entry from the front, back and roof."

"And?"

"You heard what Danny said just as good as I did."

"Tell me, anyway."

"While we wreak havoc on the inside, Johnny Blue's gonna start some fires."

"Why does the savage get to start the fires?"

"Because he don't enjoy it like the rest of us do," the second man said. "He's just gonna do his job without enjoyment."

"We ain't supposed to enjoy it?"

"No, we ain't,"

"Well . . . fuck!"

***

If the two men on the roof had maintained some distance between them, they would not have been taken so easily. As it was, they were standing side-by-side, smoking, when the two Slade men took them from behind, sliding their knives into their kidneys.

The two men slumped to the roof's surface.

"That's it!" one of the Slade men said.

***

While one of the security men walked behind the buildings, the other undid his trousers and relieved himself against a wall. He had just finished when a knife slid into him from behind. Likewise, a knife took the other security man from the back, and he slid to the ground.

***

"We supposed to do this quietly?" one of the men across the street asked the other.

"No, not quietly," the second man said. "Not quietly, at all."

As the dark of night deepened and streetlights came aglow, the two men crossed the street, stopped shy of the steps, drew their guns and pumped lead into Leo and his companion on the door.

At the sound of the shots, six more men charged the front of The Red Lady, ran up the steps and slammed into the door, causing it to fly open.

Chapter Forty-Four

Clint was outside the casino when he heard shots and the slamming of doors. It sounded to him like front and back doors.

He went into the casino, grabbed Folsom and yanked him out.

"Men to the back and the roof," he instructed.

"And you?"

"I'll handle the front door," he said. "Go!"

Folsom went for the men, while Clint ran to the front lobby. Along the way he encountered Honey Roy.

"I heard shots!" Roy shouted.

"Come with me," Clint said, "and take out that gun."

They each had their gun in hand as they reached the lobby amid more shots. One girl lay bleeding on the floor at one end, while two men lay dead at the other. Clint did a quick count of eight armed gunmen in the lobby, and started to fire, realizing he had only six shots available.

"Shoot!" he yelled at Honey Roy, hoping that two of the big man's wild shots would hit home.

***

As the eight men charged into the lobby, a girl stood in their way, and two male customers entered the lobby from the other end. Two of the gunmen shot the girl, while the others let loose on the customers, filling them with lead.

As bodies hit the ground, two men entered the lobby holding guns. One was large and the other, by description, was the Gunsmith.

This caused all eight men to pause, which turned out badly for them.

***

Clint did something he rarely did. Fanning the hammer on a gun often threw off the aim, causing the shots to go high. But Clint Adams put it to use now, fanning his pistol to cause six of the eight men to hit the floor, dead.

Honey Roy fired three times, missing with all three, so Clint holstered his gun, snatched the Peterson from Roy's large hand, and shot the other two men dead.

"Holy shit!" Honey Roy said. "I never seen shootin' like that."

"There's more shooting to be done," Clint said, dropping the Paterson and reloading his own gun. "Pick up two of those guns and watch the door. Shoot anybody you don't know, or who's not wearing a badge."

"Yessir!"

His gun fully loaded, Clint decided to run to the roof, and leave the back to Folsom and his men.

***

The two Slade men on the roof dropped down through the trap door to the top floor and heard the shots from elsewhere in the building.

"Should we go help?" one man asked.

"No," the other said. "We're charged with starting a fire. The others can handle the rest."

The first man nodded and produced a box of Lucifer stick matches.

The second man looked around the hallway they were in, then began kicking doors in until he found something that would burn.

***

When Clint reached the hallway that led to the roof, he saw two men about to set matches to a collection of broken furniture they had piled in the hall.

"I wouldn't!" he shouted.

The men looked at him and went for their guns. As Clint shot them down, their lit matches fell onto the pile of wooden furniture.

Clint rushed down the hall to kick the pile of furniture apart and stomp out whatever flames had managed to catch. He checked to make sure the two men were dead, and the embers were extinguished.

He heard shooting from elsewhere in the buildings, turned and ran toward it.

Folsom and two men ran to the rear of The Lady and caught two men who had gained entry, attempting to light matches to the wooden door.

"Hold it!" he shouted.

The two men drew their guns, turned and fired. One of Folsom's men caught a bullet in his chest, the other his shoulder. The bullets missed Folsom, who fired his own gun. His bullet struck one man, while the other managed to light the door afire. Being made of dry wood, the door erupted into flames.

The man turned to face Folsom, and both men fired. In their haste, they both missed.

Clint entered the hall from behind Folsom, gun in hand, and fired. The bullet hit Slade's man in the chest, driving him back against the burning door, and through it.

Clint stood next to Folsom.

"You hit?"

"No," Folsom said, "but the others are. Is there any-more shooting?"

They both stood and listened.

"I don't think so, but we better make sure."

They helped the two wounded men up and started making their way back to the lobby.

Chapter Forty-Five

Johnny Blue entered The Barbary Queen and went directly to the office with the bad news.

"He what?" Danny asked, after Johnny finished his story.

"He shot eight of 'em," Blue said.

Danny and Dolph exchanged glances.

"The sonofabitch!" Danny hissed.

"What now?" Dolph asked.

Danny ignored his brother and spoke to Johnny Blue.

"Are they all dead?"

"I think so."

"You don't know?"

"I did not go inside once the shooting started," Johnny Blue said. "I looked in the door and saw all the men go down. Are they all dead? It is the Gunsmith. I assume he shoots to kill. Which is why I am leaving town."

Both brothers ignored Johnny Blue's departure.

"Danny," Dolph said, "if even one is alive and talks—"

"Yes, yes," Danny said. "We can expect a visit from the Gunsmith, or the law."

"So what do we do?"

Danny didn't answer, because he didn't know.

***

When Clint and Folsom got to the lobby, they saw Detective Muldoon moving among the fallen.

Honey Roy came over to them.

"He's the law," the big man said. "I figured you'd want me to let him in."

"You did right, Roy," Clint said. "You can go back to Genevieve."

"What about these guns?" Roy asked, indicating the weapons tucked into his belt.

"Keep them," Clint said.

"Thank you,"

Honey Roy left the lobby as Muldoon walked over to Clint.

"How many of these men did you shoot?" he asked.'

"There were eight," Clint said. "I killed them all."

"All of 'em?"

Clint nodded.

"Jesus!" Muldoon said. "Did you leave any alive to name the Slades?"

"No, I didn't," Clint said, "but they don't have to know that."

***

When Clint and Muldoon walked into The Barbary Queen, the bartender averted his eyes. They walked to the bar and got his attention. Muldoon showed the man his badge.

"Where are your bosses?" he asked.

"Um, uh, in their office."

"Anybody in there with them?" Muldoon asked.

"Not that I know of."

The few gamblers who were still active at that time of night paid them no attention as they crossed the room. They entered the office without knocking. Danny Slade looked up from his desk. Dolph was not present.

"Gentlemen," Danny said. "What can I do for you?"

"One of your men gave you up, Slade," Muldoon said.

"Is that a fact?" Danny replied. "Gave me up about what?"

"You know what," Clint said. "Where's your brother?"

"He'll be along," Danny said. "He's running an errand."

"That's fine," Muldoon said. "I'll take you in, and come back for him, later."

"Take me in for what?"

"I think you know," Clint said. "You and your brother are to be taken to task for sending those men to be killed by me."

"So you're sayin' you killed them, not me." Danny said.

"They were sent by you and your brother to do damage or harm," Muldoon said, "which made it necessary for Mr. Adams to kill them. For that reason, you're both under arrest. I'll take you with me now and come for your brother later."

"And what proof do you have that me and my brother were involved?"

"The word of the one man who still lives," Muldoon said.

"I doubt that."

"Nevertheless," Muldoon said, "you'll come with me."

Danny stood.

"If I go with you, what happens to my brother?"

"Mr. Adams will wait here for him and bring him to me when he arrives."

"Alive, I hope."

"That'll be up to your brother," Clint said.

Danny pointed at Muldoon.

"Me and my brother better both get to your jail alive."

"Like Mr. Adams said," Muldoon replied. "That's up to the both of you. Let's go."

As the three of them left the office, the batwing doors swung open to admit two men, one being Dolph Slade.

With him stood Gus Hardcastle.

"Gus."

"Clint."

"I was wondering where you'd gotten off to."

"Here I am," Hardcastle said.

Activities in the Barbary Queen ceased as all eyes fell on Clint and Hardcastle.

"Gentlemen," Muldoon said. "This is not the wild West."

"Just stand aside, Detective," Clint said. "This is kind of personal."

Muldoon stood aside, keeping Danny Slade close, his hand on his gun. Dolph stepped away to put distance between him and Hardcastle.

"You've been working for the Slades this whole time?" Clint asked.

"Gus—" Danny started, but Muldoon quieted him with a look.

"I have."

"Jesus," Danny whispered, realizing they had been given up.

"You were recommended to me by Duke Farrell."

"Duke had no knowledge of my previous employment."

"Were you hired to watch me?" Clint asked, "or kill me?"

"Whichever," Hardcastle said.

"These two brothers are on their way to jail, Gus," Clint said. "If you kill me now, it's at your pleasure, not their bidding."

"I've been paid," Hardcastle said. "That means I have to do the job."

"Well," Clint said, "make your play and let's get it over with."

Without hesitation Hardcastle went for his weapon. He was fast, just not fast enough. With a sadness in his heart that it had come to this, Clint shot Hardcastle through the heart, blaming the Slades for this death, as well.

He looked at Muldoon.

"Was Hardcastle's word enough?"

"Seeing as how it was a dying statement, I'd say so."

Now he looked at the brothers.

"Move your asses. You're going to jail."

Chapter Forty-Six

It was several days later that the Slades were charged and jailed, pending trial. The security men who were killed had been buried, as well as the Slade men and Gus Hardcastle. Clint stopped by Duke Farrell's on his way out of town.

"Thought you were gonna stay and relax," Duke said.

"I've relaxed enough these past few days. It's time to go."

"Well, I'm glad you spent the last couple of days here. And I look forward to your return."

"Good to see you, Duke."

The two men shook hands and Clint turned to leave Duke's office.

"Clint."

"Yes?" Clint turned.

"I'm sorry about Hardcastle. I thought he was trust-worthy."

"He was," Clint said. "Someone just hired him first."

Clint left.

***

Clint's last stop before leaving San Francisco was The Red Lady. He dismounted outside and went up the stairs. Briefly, he thought about poor Leo as the new doorman opened the door for him. He walked down the now familiar hall to The Red Lady's office. As he entered, Delilah stood from behind the desk, wearing a red dress. There was no sign of Genevieve.

She spread her arms, smiled and said, "As promised."

Upcoming New Release

THE GUNSMITH
J.R. ROBERTS

STEEL DISASTER
BOOK 479

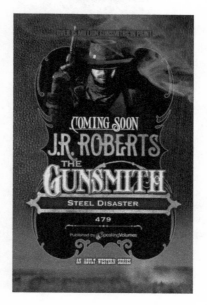

**For more information
visit:** <u>www.SpeakingVolumes.us</u>

On Sale!

THE GUNSMITH
BOOKS 430 – 477

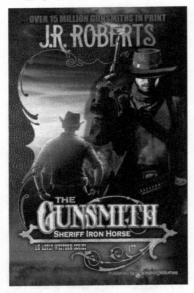

For more information
visit: <u>www.SpeakingVolumes.us</u>

On Sale!

THE GUNSMITH GIANT SERIES

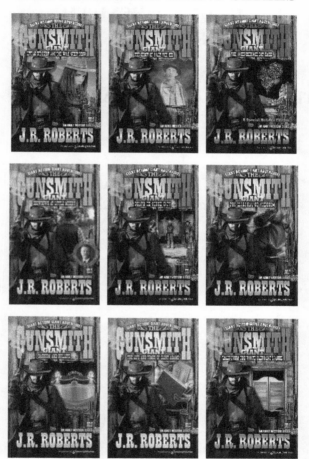

For more information
visit: www.SpeakingVolumes.us

Upcoming New Release

LADY GUNSMITH
J.R. ROBERTS

ROXY DOYLE AND
THE QUEEN OF THE PASTEBOARDS
BOOK 10

**For more information
visit**: www.SpeakingVolumes.us

On Sale!

LADY GUNSMITH
BOOKS 1 - 9

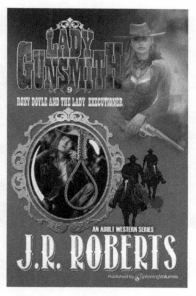

For more information
visit:

On Sale!

AWARD-WINNING AUTHOR
ROBERT J. RANDISI (J.R. ROBERTS)

For more information
visit: www.SpeakingVolumes.us

CPSIA information can be obtained
at www.ICGtesting.com
Printed in the USA
LVHW111926050922
727604LV00018B/251